"I still don't know if I'm dressed correctly."

Thinking of the lawn parties back home, she chose a fine white dress and put the boys in dark trousers and nice white shirts.

Zach ran his gaze over her length, finally meeting her eyes, a gleam making his sparkle. "I think you look very nice." He grinned. "And appropriate."

Her mouth refused to function as his gaze drew her into a land of flowers, perfume, and warmth. It wasn't until he turned his attention back to the horse that she could gather her thoughts back to the reality of Donald's weight against her arm, the hard bench pressing into her legs, and the sharp odor of the horse.

"I never paid much attention to what women wear," Zach said in a slow way, "but seems to me they dress much like you for this event." He emphasized the last word in such a way she understood him to mean it was only a picnic.

"It's not the crowning of a king?" She sounded slightly shocked.

He laughed. "Hey. Far as I know, we've never even had the Prime Minister attend. So relax and enjoy yourself."

"You're right. I intend to have a great deal of fun." She smiled to herself. Why wouldn't she? A long lazy afternoon with Zach at her side; the boys playing with their friends—it sounded idyllic.

LINDA FORD draws on her own experiences living in the Canadian prairie and Rockies to paint wonderful adventures in romance and faith. She lives in Alberta, Canada, with her family, writing as much as her full-time job of taking care of a paraplegic and four kids who are still at home will allow. Linda says, "I thank God that he has given me a full productive life and that I'm not bored. I thank Him for placing a little bit of the creative energy revealed in his creation into me, and I pray I might use my writing for his honor and glory."

Books by Linda Ford

HEARTSONG PRESENTS
HP240—The Sun Still Shines
HP268—Unchained Hearts
HP368—The Heart Seeks a Home
HP448—Chastity's Angel
HP463—Crane's Bride
HP531—Lizzie
HP547—Maryelle
HP575—Grace

Irene

Linda Ford

Heartsong Presents

*To Sien and Kelly serving the Lord as Bible translators
in Papua, New Guinea.
May you be blessed in your work.*

"...blessed when you come in and blessed when you go out."
Deuteronomy 28:6

A note from the Author:
*I love to hear from my readers! You may correspond with me
by writing:*

> **Linda Ford**
> **Author Relations**
> **PO Box 719**
> **Uhrichsville, OH 44683**

ISBN 1-59310-062-0

IRENE

*Our mission is to publish and distribute inspirational products offering
exceptional value and biblical encouragement to the masses.*

All Scripture quotations are taken from the King James Version of the
Bible.

All of the characters and events in this book are fictitious. Any resemblance to actual persons, living or dead, or to actual events is purely
coincidental.

PRINTED IN THE U.S.A.

one

Alberta, Canada, 1919

Irene Brighty took a deep, steadying breath and stepped from the train. Even before the man on the platform strode forward with the air of having a job to do and wanting to get it done, she knew it was him.

"Miss Brighty?"

Her throat tight, she extended her right hand and answered, "Yes. Zachary Marshall, I presume?"

"Call me Zach." Her hand became lost in the palm of a hand big enough to plug a small window.

He studied her frankly, and she did the same of him, silently measuring this man, seeking clues to his character. Outwardly, he was nothing like what she'd expected—that he would be like his cousin, Billy, who had married her sister, Grace, or like other members of the family she'd met in Toronto. True, he had the same dark, probing eyes and fine head of dark hair, but there the likeness ended. This man lacked the slenderness of his cousin; indeed, he was built like a stevedore, with wide shoulders and thick arms. She looked straight into his eyes without having to tilt her head either up or down and discovered she liked being the same height as he.

Irene stood straight before his scrutiny, her fingers digging into the material of her handbag as she resisted the urge to run her hand over her hair.

She wondered what he saw: A woman past her youth? The angular build of her? Her too-long face, too-square jaw, or her prominent chin? A handsome face, Father always assured her, but Irene had no disillusionments about her overly strong features. She was no prize to be carried home for display.

He jerked his head once as if to say she'd passed muster. "Are you ready?"

She liked his voice, slow and deep like water running placidly over smooth rocks. Courage returned. "I'm as ready as I can be."

He gave her a startled look.

She followed at his side, easily keeping step with him. She didn't know why it should, but that one fact filled her with reassurance, and she relaxed.

A few minutes later, she sat beside him on the hard wagon seat, her trunks stowed in the back—her whole life packed into two chests.

"I've made arrangements with Reverend Williams. We're to go directly there."

"Very good." Her voice remained firm.

He pulled up before a small frame house huddled close to the tiniest church she'd ever seen. A sign on the gate beyond read Westina Cemetery. Was this where Zach had buried his wife?

"I'm not wanting you to have any wrong notions about this marriage," Zach said, studiously keeping his gaze on his big hands from which hung the slack reins. "It's not for me I suggested we get married. It's for my boys." She saw the depth of his need and understood, too, by the set of his jaw that he would never beg.

"The loss of their mother has left them battered like a pair of old shoes. Harry—well, he tries so hard to be a man, but he's only nine years old. And Donald—he's four now and he's. . . Well, you'll see for yourself."

Irene waited quietly, letting the man say what he had to say.

"They need a secure, stable home. They can't have a continual going and coming of people." He took a slow, deep breath. "Me. Well, I want nothing more than to be left alone. I will never love another woman."

Irene touched her handbag where the letter lay crumpled, the folds starting to crack from so much handling. "A housekeeper and someone to care for your children. You made it plain in your letter. I understand the conditions, and I agree to them. You'll not find me wanting in the performance of my duties." Her mouth went dry. He had not mentioned whether he expected those duties to include the marital bed.

"If you are of a mind to give it another thought, now would be the time. Once we've had our 'I do's' said in front of the preacher, I'll not look kindly at either of us changing our minds." His eyes turned dark with intensity. "I won't be letting anyone hurt my boys."

"I'll not be changing my mind." She took a deep breath. "Perhaps you need to understand my situation. After all, if you're to become my husband. . ." She half stumbled over the word. "You deserve some sort of explanation. I've given your suggestion a lot of thought. I've prayed about it, and I'm certain this is what I want to do. You said in your letter that you were a Christian. I only want to hear you say it aloud."

"I am a believer." He stared at his hands.

"That's fine then." She paused. "And if you have a mind to change your offer, now is the time. Before we give our vows." His eyebrows lifted in question marks. "You see me. I'm an old maid. Maybe you'll be wanting to change your mind."

"Old?" He seemed genuinely surprised. "How old is old?"

She smiled at his philosophical question. "I'm twenty-eight."

A strange, deep sound rumbled in his chest. A chuckle? A grunt? Irene couldn't tell. But his expression softened. "I fear you will be shocked, then, by my age."

"No, your aunt said you were thirty-four, near as she could reckon."

"My aunt is correct."

"Seems all my life I've been caring for people. First, my sister, Grace, and my father; when the war began, I worked as a nurse in a hospital. Fix them up, get them on their feet, and wave them good-bye." Her smile trembled. "Maybe I'm a little like your boys. I'm tired of all the goings and comings."

He nodded. "Then let's get it done."

Before she could answer, he jumped from the wagon, landing

lightly. With a quick gait, as if he had springs fastened to the soles of his shoes, he strode to her side. Amazed that someone built like him could be almost buoyant, she barely managed to get to her feet before he lifted her down. The ease with which he set her on the ground beside him made her feel light and young again. A giggle tickled the back of her throat, but she restrained it, allowing only a wide smile.

He watched her, his eyebrows again asking questions, but before she could explain her smile, the door above them flew open, and a red-haired woman raced down the steps. "Hello. I'm Mrs. Williams. Etta. Call me Etta. We've been waiting for you. I'm so excited. This is so romantic. Come on in."

Zach, at Irene's side, murmured beneath the woman's chatter. "Etta Williams, preacher's wife. She's all aflutter about the arrangements."

Irene pressed her fingers to her mouth to hide her amusement. This young, wild-looking woman seemed out of place in her role.

She ushered them up the steps and into the parlor where her husband waited—a sandy-haired young man with a serious, kindly demeanor.

Then Irene forgot everything else as the preacher faced them. "Marriage is a serious institution and not to be entered into lightly." He stared hard into Irene's eyes. "I know you've only met Zach. What you're about to do is either foolish or very brave." He shook his head. "I'm not prepared to say which."

"I'm past the age of being foolish about marriage," Irene murmured. "Besides, Mr. Marshall—Zach—and I have already had this discussion. We are both sure about what we are doing."

The preacher's stern gaze shifted to the man on her right. "Is that right, Zach?"

"Get on with it, preacher boy. We're both old enough to know what we're doing. And we aren't getting any younger standing here waiting." His voice was low and lazy, like he found the whole thing vastly amusing. Well, she supposed she couldn't blame him. It was highly unusual to marry someone on first meeting.

"So long as you're both willing and have given it due consideration. . . Etta, bring me my book and call Mrs. Johnson." He turned back to Irene and Zach as Etta hurried from the room. "I asked Mrs. Johnson to be the second witness."

He took the book his wife offered; Etta stood beside Irene, an older woman hovered on the far side of Zach, then the preacher began, "Do you Zachary Marshall. . ."

Zach's hand engulfed Irene's, as if to let her know that although only a marriage of convenience, he intended to take his responsibilities seriously.

As did she.

"I now pronounce you man and wife. You may salute the bride."

Zach's grip tightened; his dark eyes glistened with purpose as he pulled her close and touched her lips in a fleeting kiss.

Irene didn't even have time to close her eyes.

She pressed her tongue against her top teeth. The unexpected acknowledgment of their status as man and wife touched her in a way she could not have anticipated, filling her heart with a quivering, unfamiliar emotion.

Then they were in the wagon, heading west out of town.

Westina lay nestled in a hollow between rolling hills dotted with groves of trees exuberant in new spring growth. The road climbed gently as they left town. Since leaving Calgary, Irene had been drawn to the view. Mountains distant and stark, crowned with glistening snow, saw-toothed the horizon.

"Oh," she gasped, as they crested the hill. The mountains no longer were the horizon; they were half the sky. "I feel like I can reach out and touch them." She filled her lungs with the cool, sweet air.

"You like the sight?"

"Very much. I can't get over how majestic they are."

"Then I think you'll like the farm. We have a great mountain view."

"Then I know I shall enjoy it." She sighed her pleasure. "I could never get tired of a view like this."

He nodded. "Stirs a man's heart."

"Yes, exactly." His poetic words, plainly spoken, pleased her. She'd seen enough of brash young soldiers overimpressed with their own wonder. "What else will I like about the farm?"

Again, that sound, deep in his chest. Was it amusement or derision?

"Depends on what sorts of things please you."

"I suppose you could say I like plain, simple things. I like the morning air when it is cool and sweet. I like the mad display of color at sunset." She gave a brisk chuckle. "And as you can tell, I like the sound of my own voice."

"Don't apologize. We have a great deal of learning to do, one about the other. Continue. Please."

She shifted about, trying to find a position that relieved the hardness of the bench and finding none, leaned against her hands. "What else do I like? I like the smell of fresh baking and a clean house. I like taking care of people. I like walking in the cool of the evening. I like order." She stopped, finding it difficult to tell a stranger so much about herself. A stranger? Her husband. It didn't bear a lot of thinking about at the moment. She had made up her mind, and now she would face the future bravely. "How about you? What sorts of things do you like and dislike?"

He stared straight ahead; the way his lips tightened were the only indication he'd heard her.

She waited, sensing he'd never given the idea much thought.

"Don't think much about what I like or don't like. Mostly I just do what needs doing."

"An admirable quality. 'Joy's soul is in the doing.' It's something I remember from school."

"Well said."

Zach seemed lost in thought. Irene could think of nothing more than what waited for her at the end of this journey.

"Are the boys prepared for my coming?"

"I've told them they're getting a new mama."

Mama. She rolled the word around in her mind. "How did they respond?"

He stretched his legs out. "Harry only asked for how long."

Irene frowned. "I don't understand."

Zach fixed her with a hard, glittering look. "He was asking how long you'd be their mother. In their experience, even mothers don't stay around long."

"Oh, I see." She met his look as equally hard and determined as he. "Then I hope you assured them this mother is here to stay."

"I think that would be up to you." His gaze never faltered.

"Quite so. I'll see to it."

Zach turned away. "This is the turnoff."

Irene perched on the edge of the bench, wanting to see everything at once.

The road ducked between tall spruce trees, dark with winter's sleep. Bright green of deciduous trees winked around the dark evergreens. The air danced with the spicy, sharp scent of poplar trees.

The road curved and opened to a meadow. A low cottage lay to the right; behind it, the top of a hip-roofed barn.

Zach stopped the wagon and pointed away from the buildings. She gasped. They faced a sweeping valley that rose to glistening, rugged mountains. "I've never seen anything so beautiful," she whispered. "I can't imagine waking up to this every morning."

"It's the best view in the country. The table is placed in front of a window so we can see the mountains while we eat."

Her heart had never been so full. The awe-inspiring view was a vivid reminder of God's strength and power. No matter what the future held, one glance at the mountains would be enough to sustain her.

Zach slapped the reins, jolting the wagon onward. "The boys are waiting."

Irene smiled. "No more than I."

As they approached the house, the door opened and a young woman, dark and slender with a striking resemblance to Billy back east, stepped out with two little boys ahead of her.

Irene tried to study them without staring.

Zach stopped the wagon, jumped to the ground, and again lifted her down.

Her glance slid past his shoulder to the trio on the step.

Zach led her to the young woman. "Irene, this is my sister, Addie. Addie Adams."

"Welcome, Irene. We've been waiting anxiously for you."

Zach pulled the boys toward him. "This is Harry and Donald. Boys, say hello to your new mama."

Harry, his brown hair damp and slicked down like his aunt had recently instructed him to tidy up, held out his small hand. "Hello," he said, his light brown eyes troubled. With his other hand, he held tightly to his little brother.

"This young man is Donald." Zach touched the child's shoulder protectively.

"Hello, Donald." Dark eyes, dark hair—the child was very much like his father in looks. He sucked three fingers of one hand, his dark eyes regarding her.

"Come in. I've made supper," Addie said.

Zach restrained the boys, his huge hands on their shoulders. "The boys will help me unload the wagon."

Irene stepped into a large kitchen; the table was pushed close to the window as Zach had said.

"You've got your job cut out for you here." Addie studied her.

Irene shrugged out of her jacket and hung it on a hook behind the door before she answered. "What do you mean?"

Addie indicated the trio by the wagon. "Them. All of them. Seems like they can't find their way back home."

"Home?"

"I don't mean here." Addie's arm swept the air to indicate the room. "I mean here." She pressed a palm to her chest. "Poor little Donald. He hasn't said a word since his mother passed away. And Harry—I worry about Harry. He is far too serious for a child his age. It's like he's afraid if he relaxes, his world will shatter. Sit down. I'm sure you're tired."

"Thank you. Overwhelmed more than tired."

"Zach, he's changed a great deal, too," Addie continued. "There's no life left in him. Except where the boys are concerned." She shook her head. "The three of them, so hurt. I don't know if they'll ever get over it. I know it's only six months since Esther died, but they're still so shattered by it all." She scooped mashed potatoes into a bowl and poured gravy into a jug.

Zach strode in with a trunk on his shoulder. When he brought in the second trunk, the boys followed him.

"Supper is served," Addie announced.

The two boys pressed themselves against Zach's leg. Zach scooped Donald into his arms. "I guess we should get washed up, right, boys?" He took them to the washstand.

Irene watched the gentle way he took each pair of hands and rubbed them together, then checked to make sure they had dried carefully. He took the corner of the towel and swiped a streak from Harry's face. "Good enough."

Irene felt the boys' gazes on her.

"How was your trip?" Addie asked.

"It was long. Canada is a big country, but I enjoyed the scenery. Particularly the last day with the mountains to look at." She shifted her gaze toward Harry. "Just as we crossed into Alberta I saw these little deerlike creatures that raced alongside the train for several miles." Harry's eyes grew wide. "The conductor said they were antelope. Prairie creatures. He said God made them with something special so they could outrun their enemies." She waited, wanting to see if Harry would express any interest. "Do you know what that special thing is?"

Harry edged to the front of his chair. "What?"

"The conductor said that antelope have a very large windpipe that enables them to suck in lots of air so they can run fast for a long time."

Harry's gaze shifted to his father. "You ever seen antelope, Dad?"

"No, I haven't, but I'd like to."

Harry turned shyly to Irene. "We've seen a mommy moose and her baby down by the river. And we got baby kittens."

Donald turned toward Harry, and although Donald never spoke, Harry said, "Donald found them first."

"Will I be invited to see them?"

Harry and Donald exchanged glances, then Harry said, "We'll take you."

"Thank you. I can hardly wait."

When supper was over, Zach pushed back from the table. "I need to do the chores."

Harry scooted from the table. Donald stuck his fingers in his mouth and trotted after him, but Zach intercepted him.

"You could stay with Aunt Addie, Son." But Donald gave his father a hard look, and Zach relented. "Get your jacket and come with us, then."

Addie waited until the door closed before she turned to Irene. "I'll show you around, then I best be getting home and looking after my own man."

"I appreciate your help." Irene followed her into the next room, a parlor with a worn burgundy sofa and wooden rocker, a box of toys near the chair, and a table with a mantel clock.

Addie led the way back through the kitchen to another door that entered a short, square hallway with a row of hooks overloaded with coats and scarves on one wall, a large wooden chest beneath the coats. Two doors faced each other.

"The boys sleep here." Addie stepped into the left door. "I've cleaned up some. I didn't think it was fair for you to walk into a big mess." She pointed to the other door. "This is the other bedroom."

Irene's gaze took in the wide bed and high dresser, her trunks against one wall.

"I'll stay until the boys are ready for bed." Addie gathered up dishes to wash. "Unless you'd feel better if I left."

"No, I appreciate your help. There's so much I need to learn all at once. Where things are kept, what the boys like, who they are, what Zach expects. . ." She bit her bottom lip.

Addie, as Zach's sister, might think Irene indiscreet.

Addie smiled gently. "Even Zach doesn't know what Zach wants."

Irene chuckled. "I've had the same feeling once or twice myself."

"Life gets far too complicated at times," Addie said. "But then why should that surprise us? My mother always said, 'Life is so full of the unexpected that sometimes I think the unexpected is really the expected.'" She laughed. "I'm sure I don't know what she meant, but it sounds wonderfully wise."

Irene laughed with her. "It's a mercy we can't see what lies ahead. I'm afraid it would make us unable to enjoy what the present offers."

"That's a fact. Who would marry if they thought they would have to go through what Zach has gone through—is going through." She shuddered. "If I thought I'd ever lose Pete, why, I don't know what I'd do. Fortunately, we only have to live one day at a time. Now, you'll be needing to know where all the fixings are. There's a lovely big pantry here." She led the way into a narrow room, its shelves filled with every assortment of bottled goods and baking supplies. "Zach and the boys will eat most anything."

At that moment, Zach and the boys clattered through the door, pails banging, boots thudding. He bent and helped Donald with his jacket. When he straightened, his eyes sought Irene. Was he wondering if anything had made her change her mind? She smiled. "Addie's been showing me around."

"I thought I'd get the boys ready for bed," Addie said.

"It's been a long day. I suppose you fellows are tired," he said.

Harry shook his head. "Can't we play for awhile?"

"Not tonight, Son. It's been a long day for all of us." His voice was gentle yet firm, and he ran his hand over the boy's hair. "Run and get your pajamas on."

Harry nodded, reaching for Donald.

"I'll help Donald get ready. You bring me his pajamas." Zach lifted Donald into his arms and sank into the chair next to Irene. The little boy snuggled into his father's neck with the assurance of a young pup at its mother's side. His dark eyes regarded Irene, his fingers were secured in his mouth.

Irene's throat tightened. It was a pose so protective, so sheltering that she could almost feel the child's tension ease.

Harry returned in a pair of pajamas several inches too short, and the front bunched up where he'd tried to fix a tear with a safety pin. The idea of this child struggling to do for himself what should be done for him filled her with admiration even as tears burned at the back of her nose.

"Here, Donald." Harry put a pair of threadbare pajamas on the table. He untied Donald's shoes, struggled with a knot in the laces, pulled off the shoes and socks, and set them on the table.

Zach set Donald forward. "Time to get rid of that shirt." He eased it over Donald's head, waiting for Donald to momentarily take his fingers from his mouth, then slipped the pajama shirt on with deftness that made Irene smile.

Addie chuckled. "He's got that down pat."

Irene nodded. "Looks like a man with lots of practice."

Donald settled again into the hollow of Zach's leg. "Man learns to do any job efficiently," Zach said to Addie.

"Like a woman doesn't!" Addie protested.

"Women fuss over little things." He half smiled at Irene when Addie sputtered.

"Little things. Like what?" Seeing his grin, she laughed. "You sucker me in every time. You'd think I'd learn."

"You'd think so, but I'm doubtful."

"You're doubtful? Why. . ." She swallowed the rest. "Why, you're despicable."

Irene laughed. She sensed the deep affection between the brother and sister, affection that allowed for teasing, and a shared strength, she guessed, that would see either one come to the rescue of the other.

Addie rose. "I think I'll head on home before it gets dark."

"Better get on home before Pete comes gunning for me."

Zach nodded. "Thanks for your help."

"Anytime. I mean that." She turned to Irene. "I'm only a couple miles away if you need anything. I wish you all the best." She nodded to Zach. "I believe she'll do just fine." She kissed each boy. "You boys behave yourselves, or I'll be back."

Harry giggled.

Then she was gone.

The four of them sat around the table, not looking at each other; the only sound was Donald sucking on his fingers.

"Come on, boys, time to climb into bed."

Irene wanted to offer to read to them, but she knew it was too soon. The boys needed time to get to know her. She shamelessly listened to the murmur of Zach's deep voice as he tucked them into bed and Harry's thin, childish tones as he said his prayers. Her heart swelled with unshed tears. This home had seen more than its share of sorrow and pain. As Addie had said, she had her work cut out for her in trying to help them. She knew why God had led her to this place; this family needed understanding and patience as they healed.

She longed to begin unpacking her trunks, but uncertain if Zach would want to sit at the table longer, visit in the parlor, or head for the bedroom, she remained where she was. She had no idea if Zach went to bed early or sat up late. She had no idea of what came next.

two

While she waited, Irene watched out the window knowing she would never get tired of the sight of those great, rugged mountains. The sun crowned them with a brilliant gold, then dropped behind the jagged peaks, leaving behind a cloud of pink. She breathed deeply as if to inhale the beauty.

She felt Zach step into the room and stiffened, wondering what was next.

He stood behind her, not speaking, until finally she felt compelled to turn and ask, "Are they settled?"

Zach, his arms crossed, his expression thoughtful, nodded. "Harry takes awhile to settle, but Donald is curled up already asleep." He pulled out a chair at the end of the table. "What do you think?"

Her mind on the sunset, her thoughts scrambled for his meaning. "Of what?"

"The boys."

"Why, they're delightful. Harry is so grown-up. And Donald—"

"He hasn't spoken since his mother died."

"I know. Addie told me. But he's still charming. His eyes say things without the need of words. Why, with eyes like that, he'd melt anyone's heart." Donald's eyes were a duplication of Zach's dark gaze. She gulped and ducked her head, afraid she'd said too much. "But. . ." She sought the right way to say what she felt.

"But what?" His words carried a hard warning note.

"I think it will take time for us to get to know each other. All of us. To understand what each one needs. To trust each other."

His shoulders relaxed. "Time is on our side."

"I hope you'll be patient with me while I learn my way

18

around." A smile tugged at her lips. "I'm used to making my own decisions, finding my own solution for problems. I'm not noted for sitting back quietly and demurely, so if I inadvertently tread on your toes, don't be afraid to speak out. I'm not intentionally abrupt."

He studied her quietly, his eyes dark and intense. Then he gave a slow smile that drove away the tension around his mouth. "I'll be letting you know if you step out-of-bounds." He chuckled. "Now I sound like a slave driver. And I'm not."

The transformation in him when he laughed sent tremors along her arms. Why, he was as handsome as could be, and the way his eyes blazed was enough to make her blink.

He pushed to his feet, forcing her to tip her head back to meet his eyes. "I've some things I need to check on outside. Go ahead and attend to your unpacking. Make yourself at home. Don't wait up for me." He strode from the house.

Irene sat back. It was a bit like getting run over by a wagon. But her trunks waited, so she lit a lantern and hurried to the bedroom.

Zach had emptied the drawers in a tall chiffonier. She unlocked the trunk containing her summer things and lifted them into the drawers. Zach's things in the wide wardrobe took little space, and she hung up her dresses and coat beside them. Her Bible and pictures of Father and of Grace and Billy's wedding, she placed on the small table by the bed. A pair of boots on one side of the bed made her choose the opposite side.

She wasn't afraid; she wasn't nervous, but not knowing what to expect from this part of the arrangement set her on edge as she prepared for bed. She lay waiting, stiff and tense. Zach did not appear. Perhaps he intended to give her plenty of time to perform her bedtime rituals, in which case, she would continue with some of her long-established habits. She picked up her Bible to read a few verses, then spent several minutes in prayer asking for wisdom and guidance in her new role.

Still he did not appear. She turned the lantern down and

lay staring at the soft shadows on the ceiling, listening as one of the boys moaned.

Her eyelids grew heavy. She forced her eyes wide open, determined to be awake when Zach came to bed. This, too, was part of the arrangement between them, and the sooner they established their roles, the better she'd like it. Not knowing was almost killing her.

A sound in the kitchen jarred her awake. It took a moment for her to remember where she was and another to decide the sound was the outside door opening and closing.

Again, she forced her eyelids up and waited.

Darkness had deepened when she awoke with a start. The lantern still burned; the bed beside her remained empty.

She struggled from her warm sleep and shrugged into her wrap. She found him in the parlor, his head against the back of the sofa, his legs stuck out awkwardly. She studied him a moment then went back to the bedroom and got a blanket. He stirred only enough to sigh as she tucked it around his shoulders.

She watched him sleep, his features indistinct in the darkness. No doubt he'd be stiff and sore in the morning. This was not how things should be. She needed to think what she should do about it.

Irene woke at first light and hurried to the kitchen. As quietly as possible, she built the fire and put coffee to boil. The aroma began to percolate through the room as Zach staggered from the parlor, his eyes bleary with sleep. The poor man looked in no condition to hear what she had to say.

"Good morning," she said, handing him a cup of coffee.

"Huh." His grunt revealed nothing about his emotional state, only a desperate need for coffee. He downed the first cupful without regard for the temperature, and she refilled the cup. Slowly, like winding up a blind, she watched him come to life.

"Looks like a nice day," he commented, staring out the window.

Irene nodded. "Not a cloud in the sky."

Finally, he set down his cup and looked at her. "Did you sleep well?"

"Fine. And yourself?"

He only gave her a hard stare.

"I'll be needing a saw today."

"A saw? What for?"

Her jaw tightened as she faced him. "I'll be sawing the bed in half today. I'll have one half, you the other."

His mouth dropped open. "Are you crazy?"

"I'll not be driving a man from his bed."

He blinked but said nothing.

She persisted. "Would you be so kind as to bring me a saw after breakfast?"

"You'd do it, wouldn't you?"

"I would, indeed."

He shook his head. "Lady, you are crazy."

"Will you get me a saw, or do I have to find it on my own?" She refused to pull back from his dark, hard look.

He held up his hand. "No need to be hasty. If you're going to force me to sleep in a bed, I'd just as soon sleep in a whole one."

She nodded. "Fine then. So long as we understand each other."

He studied her, his eyes narrow, questioning. "You don't need to think—"

"Is it morning?" Harry's question interrupted Zach's words, and he turned to his son.

"Good morning. Where's Donald?"

"I'll get him." Harry turned back down the hall.

Irene waited, but Zach did not finish what he'd started to say. What warning had he been about to deliver? She had a good idea he had been about to tell her there were things he wouldn't be pushed into doing. Which suited her just fine.

Harry returned, holding Donald firmly by the hand.

"Harry, get dressed and help me with the chores."

Harry turned, Donald still firmly attached.

"Donald can stay in the house."

Both boys jerked to a halt. Donald's wide, dark gaze stared at his father. Harry looked at his younger brother, then back to his dad.

"Do as I say, Son." Zach's voice was quiet and insistent.

Harry nodded and pulled his hand from Donald's, his expression pain-filled as he went to put on his jacket.

Donald sucked on his fingers, his eyes accusing his father as he faced him alone.

Zach scooped him up. "It's all right, little man. You can stay here with your new mommy. She needs someone to help her." Zach set Donald on his feet, and he and Harry hurried from the house without a backward look. Irene understood this was difficult for them.

The child faced Irene, his dark eyes unblinking, his lips tight around his fingers.

Irene smiled at his tiny resistance. "I guess I should make some breakfast." She purposely waited. "You got any notion what I should make?" She again waited, hoping the child would make some motion of acknowledgment besides the vigorous sucking of his fingers.

After several minutes of staring at each other, he nodded.

"Good. Is it a secret?"

Donald shook his head. His eyes darted to the pantry, then back to Irene.

"Can you show me?"

He slid into the pantry, Irene following.

"It's in here?"

He nodded.

"Can you show me where?"

His gaze never left hers.

"Ah. It's a guessing game." She thought she detected an answering gleam in his eyes. "Very well." She picked up a can of baking soda. "Is this it?"

He shook his head.

"This?" She indicated a jar of peaches. His eyes definitely

gleamed this time. "Well, why not? I'd like peaches for breakfast. Anything else?"

His gaze darted along the shelves, and he nodded.

Again she touched item after item until she reached the bag of oats. "This?"

He nodded.

"Porridge and peaches?"

He nodded.

"Very well." He followed her from the pantry. "I'll put these oats to boil right away. You know the best way to cook them is to put them on the night before and let them steam all night. But we'll make do this way today." She stood in the center of the kitchen. "Now, where do you suppose I would find the proper pot?"

Donald moved to the front of the cupboard where Irene knew the pots hung.

"You're a big help. I don't know how I'd manage without you. Now if there's anything I've forgotten, you be sure to tell me. All right?"

He nodded solemnly, watching as she set the porridge to simmer, then set the table.

"There. That's about as much as we can do until Harry and your dad get back from chores. What should we do now?"

He met her eyes.

"I know. I'll help you get dressed." She sensed his sudden withdrawal but ignored it. "But you'll have to show me where everything is and what you like to wear." She headed for the bedroom.

He hesitated a moment, then followed.

Keeping up her constant chatter, she selected a shirt and trousers for him and found a clean pair of socks. "I think I'll have to see about doing some laundry today." She cocked her head to one side and faced him, her hands on her hips. "You ever done laundry before?"

He shook his head.

"Then I guess we'll have to learn together."

Again, his eyes gleamed.

She began to pull the pajama top over his head and discovered she had to lift each arm and ease it from the sleeve while he stood as motionless and uncooperative as a little wooden toy.

She put on almost clean pants and fixed his shoes and socks. All the time he stared straight ahead, his eyes never blinking, his expression never changing.

"There." She patted his knee. "All buttons and bows."

His gaze never shifted.

A lump formed in her throat. She knelt in front of him, intercepting his gaze. His pupils narrowed as he focused on her.

"I'm just a funny-looking stranger who talks in a funny way, aren't I?"

She was almost certain he nodded.

"That's it. I knew there was some reason you didn't want to talk to me. It's my funny accent." She drew her mouth flat and said in her best cockney accent, "How much rain falls on the plain in Spain in the summertime?"

He tightened his lips, and she couldn't be certain if it was from acknowledgment of her silliness or something else. He seemed so full of fear and uncertainty. Her heart shed a tear, then she smiled at the child.

"Well, there you go. I've always been good at talking, and it seems you're very good at listening. I expect we'll do just fine."

The outer door squeaked, and Donald marched out of the room, Irene on his heels.

Zach carried a pail of foaming milk, and Harry cradled four eggs in his hands.

Harry immediately looked for Donald, as if to see whether his younger brother had survived their brief separation.

Behind his eldest son, Zach watched the boys. "Harry, get the jars for the milk," he said. "Where's the straining cloth?"

Harry deposited the eggs on top of the cupboard and lifted a two-gallon jar from underneath. "The cloth is hanging outside." He slipped past his dad to get it.

Zach met Irene's gaze. He tipped his head toward Donald

and lifted his eyebrows in question marks. Understanding his unspoken question, she nodded. "Donald helped me make breakfast," she said.

Zach smiled. "Good boy."

Donald pressed against his father's leg.

Harry returned and, with an air of experience, held the cloth over the jars while Zach poured the milk through.

"I can't get over the abundance you Canadians have. So much of everything and everything so big."

"Everything?" Harry whispered.

She nodded, pleased she had captured his attention. "Look at all that milk. I can't remember the last time I had fresh milk back in England. And eggs. We were rationed one egg a week for each person."

"One egg a week?" Harry looked as if she had suggested he could only eat once a week.

"That's all."

"You want to have some really fresh milk?" Zach asked, pouring some strained milk into a glass and handing it to her.

She drank it, exploring the taste. "I've never had milk warm from the cow before." She licked her lips. "It's different, but it's good."

"What other things?" Harry asked.

Irene returned the glass to the counter and smiled her thanks at Zach. "Why, things like your gardens. They're miles big. Your fields go on and on." She waved toward the window. "The mountains fill the sky. Everything is so big." Her gaze lighted on Zach's hands as he covered the bottles of milk. "Why, even people are bigger. Look at your father's hands. I've never before seen such fine, big hands."

His big hands stopped. Sudden silence rang with surprise.

She felt Zach's gaze upon her. "I'm sorry. I didn't mean to be so personal."

For a moment, he didn't speak. Then he nodded, a slight gleam in his eyes. "Is this one of those times you warned me about?"

It was her turn to look surprised.

"Last night. Didn't you warn me—"

She grimaced. "That I might trod on toes. There's no need to tell me I've stepped out-of-bounds."

He held her gaze. "You haven't trod on my toes. I know I have ham hock hands. They're good for work, but not much to look at. I'm flattered you think them fine." He turned back to his task, and she hugged to her heart the wonderful feeling of having touched him. Not physically, but emotionally.

Over breakfast, she said, "You best be telling me what you favor for mealtimes. Donald helped me with breakfast, but he's a bit reticent."

"What's 'retsent' mean?" Harry asked.

"It means he's a man of few words."

Harry nodded, then a flicker of a smile crossed his lips. "No words, you mean."

"I told him I didn't blame him for not wanting to confide in a total stranger. And they don't come much stranger than me, do they?" She laughed. "Strange accent, strange habits. Why, I'd guess you're right now thinking, 'she's about the strangest bird I ever saw.' Aren't you?"

Zach looked startled by her nonsense, but Harry smiled. "You're not a bird. You're too big."

Irene watched Donald's gaze shift back and forth from his brother to Irene. This boy didn't miss anything.

She grinned at Harry. "And I don't lay eggs. At least I never have yet."

Harry giggled, and for a heartbeat, Donald let his fingers drop from his mouth.

Irene smiled at the three of them. "But not to worry. I'm sure you'll get used to me soon enough, and things will be all buttons and bows."

Harry's eyebrows knit together. "Buttons and bows?"

"One of my funny expressions. I suppose it means everything is all fixed up with all the proper buttons and bows. It means everything will be all right."

Harry nodded.

Zach handed Donald his spoon. "Finish your breakfast, Son."

They finished up, and Irene gathered the dirty dishes. Zach leaned back in his chair, watching her.

She found his concentrated study unsettling but carried on as if she wasn't aware of it, wondering if his thoughts included doubts about his decision. No doubt she'd already managed to challenge his idea of a proper wife. But she couldn't help who she was, and although she worked hard on curbing her tongue and speaking her mind in love, sometimes she said and did things that would have been better left unsaid and undone.

"Would you like a tour of the farm?"

His offer was so far removed from her own thoughts that she almost dropped the dish she held. "I certainly would."

Harry took Donald's hand and led him outside. Zach waited for Irene.

"It's only a small farm," he said, almost apologetically. Yet she caught a note of strong pride as he added, "but it's productive. We'll never go hungry living here."

As she stepped from the house, she stopped, her eyes seeking the mountain peaks.

He waited as if he understood her need to look at the view.

"I'll show you the barn first," he said when she sighed and turned her attention back to him.

The boys marched ahead with all the confidence of knowing their boundaries.

At the barn, Zach threw open a wide door and stood aside for Irene to enter. She stepped into the dusty shadows. The pungent odor of animal manure stung her nose. Shafts of light sliced through the floating dust motes. Overall prevailed the sweet, spicy, smell of hay.

Harry and Donald entered a small stall, empty except for harnesses and buckets.

Zach hung back, his practiced gaze running along the stalls on either side of the alleyway. Finally, his gaze rested on Irene. "I've had to take Donald with me when we do chores.

Harry's big enough to help and quick enough to get out of the way if something goes wrong. Donald is too little, but I've had no choice."

Irene nodded. "What else could you do?"

Zach continued. "I know he won't like it, but I don't want him to have to come with us all the time."

She heard the mixture of emotions in his voice, concern both for the child's safety and his tender feelings when he understood Donald might feel left out.

"He'll miss being with you, but once he learns you'll be back as soon as you're done, he'll accept it. I'll do my best to keep him happily amused."

Zach smiled. "I'm glad you understand." His look of gratitude made her want to speak a world of assurances.

"It will be all buttons and bows. You'll see."

He chuckled, a deep-throated sound that did strange things to her insides. "Buttons and bows, eh? Sounds prissy to me."

It was her turn to laugh. "Look at the four of us. Do any of us look like we stand a chance at being prissy?" She nodded toward the boys, who were sitting in a manger, hay clinging to their clothes. "Prissy would hardly be romping in a hay manger. Me. . ." She pretended to dust her clothes. "Practical. Functional. But prissy? No." She tipped her head as if seeing him for the first time. "As for you." She searched for the right word. "I'd say powerful, even stubborn, but definitely not prissy. Never."

His unblinking gaze made her think of Donald. Something dark and mysterious crossed his eyes. Had she touched a sore spot? Or had she been too bold for his liking? Before she could retract her words or offer an explanation, he turned toward the empty stalls.

"The horses and cows are out grazing right now. They're glad to see spring and green grass."

She gratefully accepted the shift in conversation. What explanation could she offer? She had no idea why she kept saying such personal things to him. Despite being married, they were strangers. Yet there was something about him that left her slightly unraveled around the edges.

She ran her finger along the smooth plank of the gate. What did she expect? Strangers, yet married. What rules of conduct governed such a situation? "I'm awfully glad for spring, too. I thought the war would never end," she added, surprising herself by her sudden change of topic.

He leaned against the gate to study her. "Was it really awful for you?"

She shrugged. "The injured kept coming and coming. Some of them mere boys. Feet rotted off from the wet they stood in day after day. Infected wounds. And worse." She clamped her lips together. She didn't dare start recalling the dreadful things she'd seen, or she'd never quit. She was quite certain the last thing this man needed was a recital of the horrors of war.

He touched her hand where it lay on the top plank. "I'm sorry."

His touch drove back the ghosts. Her smile shaky, she nodded. "Weren't you in the war?"

He grimaced. "I only got as far as Newfoundland where I was training as a mechanic." A dark shadow crossed his face. "They sent me home when my wife died." His face was a mask.

She touched his arm, surprised at its solidness and bulk. His muscle twitched beneath her palm. "I'm sorry." Her heart overflowed with pain at what this family had been through; words seemed so hollow. "I'm so sorry."

He lifted his head, looking behind Irene. "Come on, boys."

Harry's muffled voice answered, "We want her to see the baby kittens."

"I'd love to." She raised her eyebrows, waiting for Zach to give his permission.

"You might as well."

She hurried back to the stall where the boys sat in the hay, a shaggy cat purring loudly as they petted her babies. Irene had never seen such tiny creatures. "They're sweet. Can I pick one up?"

Harry chose a black one and handed it to her.

She lifted the tiny thing to her face. "Its eyes are closed."

"You've never seen newborn kittens, have you?" Zach's expression showed amusement.

"They're born with their eyes shut," Harry explained patiently.

Irene laughed. "I suppose I knew that. How old are they?"

Harry looked toward his father. "How old?"

"About a week."

"Donald found them." Harry pointed to his brother.

"Good for you."

The boy's fingers returned to his mouth, and she restrained a shudder at all the dirt that went with them.

Zach extracted Donald from his nest. "Come along, now." He brushed the hay from the child.

Irene helped Harry to his feet and dusted him off. "You've got hay all over you." She picked bits from his hair. "What you're needing is a good shaking off." She roughed her hands over him until he laughed. Pleased, she straightened. "That's better."

Zach closed the door behind them and set Donald on his feet. Harry immediately took his hand, and they ran along the pole fence.

"I have eight horses and twenty cows." Zach's voice deepened with pride as he pointed out the animals grazing along the tree line. "Do you ride?"

"No, I've never had the chance."

"You'll learn."

"Is that a promise or an order?" She kept her eyes on the animals but knew he drew back, probably surprised at her directness.

"I didn't mean for it to sound like an order. Guess I'm too used to telling the boys what to do. I'm sorry."

She faced him. "No, it's I who should be sorry. I shouldn't be so prepared to feel I have to defend myself."

They considered each other for several seconds, the morning light drawing hard planes across his features until he smiled and softened the landscape. "Seems we have a great deal to learn of each other."

"Wasn't it you who said we have lots of time?"

They fell into step, walking the length of the pole fence. "All the time we need."

His words flowed through her, comforting, strengthening. . .

"You can see the fields from here." He stopped at the end of the fence.

She saw a yellowed field and another ridged with raw earth.

"It's time I was plowing, but I haven't known what to do with the boys. I'm glad you're here in time for spring work."

He truly sounded glad, no doubt because it freed him to get on with the farming. Nevertheless, she let herself enjoy the sound of his pleasure. "I'm glad to be here in time to help you."

Again they faced each other, searching for clues as to hidden meanings, true feelings, and what the future held. He plucked a bit of hay from her hair. "Not very prissy," he murmured.

His touch did unfamiliar things to her nerve endings, making them dance in an alarming fashion. She took a deep breath, forcing her emotions into submission—something she had much experience in doing—and reminded herself their marriage was a matter of convenience only.

He turned back, past the barn, to the chicken coop with a high wire fence. "The hens are laying good again."

"Whatever that means."

He chuckled. "I keep forgetting you aren't a farm girl. Hens don't lay much during winter. So you see," he said, fixing his dark gaze on her, "we didn't have a lot of eggs for awhile but never rationed like you."

She nodded. "Everything was rationed. We had to feed the army, you know."

"Thankfully, it's over. The war to end all wars."

"Amen."

Again, Irene felt she had touched a receptive nerve in the man, and it warmed her to know they shared common ideals.

Their steps brought them full circle to the house.

"I didn't see a garden." Irene knew a garden was essential.

"I'll show you the spot." He led her behind the house to a fenced enclosure overgrown with the stalks of dead weeds almost as high as the gate. The ground looked damp and stubborn.

"Oh," was all she said.

"There was no garden last year."

"Of course."

He heaved a loud sigh. "I'll try to get at it soon."

Saying nothing, she turned to follow when wide, green leaves caught her attention in one corner of the garden. "Something is growing."

He turned back. "Rhubarb."

"It's pie plant, isn't it?"

"I've heard it called that."

She opened the gate and picked her way through the weeds and mud to the plant—in fact, three plants with long, reddish stems. "It looks healthy enough."

"Hard to kill rhubarb."

She nodded, her mind busy with possibilities. "Do you have a knife?"

"What for?"

She yanked stems from the ground. "I'm going to use this."

He hesitated, then crossed to her side. "Boys, come and help." He chopped off the leaves and piled stems in Harry's arms. "You could help, too, Donald, but it will take two hands."

Donald studied his brother, then gave his father a considering look. For a moment, Irene thought he would refuse; then he popped his fingers out and, imitating Harry, held his arms out to receive the stems. "There you go. Harry will put them on the counter for you."

The boys headed for the house.

"That's enough for today," Irene said, wiping her hands on a hanky.

Zach waited at the gate as she picked her way back across the garden.

"I'll leave the boys with you while I ride out and check the pasture fences."

"We'll be fine."

"All buttons and bows?"

She laughed. "Perhaps. Will you tell the boys?"

"I will."

They paused at the door. She could tell he had something on his mind.

She met his gaze frankly. "What is it? Are you worried about the boys?"

He nodded, a troubled look racing across his face. "I don't want anything to happen to them."

She knew what he meant. Life had been far too hard already. Even the least unkindness to them would be unfair. She touched his arm. "Zach, I may be brusque and outspoken. I may even be guilty of putting my foot in my mouth on occasion, but I have never been accused of unkindness." She took a deep breath. "Your boys are safe with me." She gave a crooked grin. "Who knows? They might even enjoy themselves."

"I don't mean to accuse you of incompetence. Or worse. It's only that they've been through so much."

She squeezed his arm. "No need to explain. Of course you're concerned. I admire that."

He mumbled something, but she didn't catch it. Something about blame or shame? Before she could ask him, he went inside to explain to the boys that he was going.

three

Zach hurried out, his expression tight. Despite her assurance the boys would be fine with her, she knew he found it difficult to leave them for even a few hours.

She faced the pair. They stood at the table behind long stalks of rhubarb. "Well, I think we better get to work if we're to get a pie made for dinner; I'll be needing some help." She looked around the room. "I wonder where I could find a couple pairs of hands to help me?"

Harry nodded, his expression serious. "We could help you."

She clasped her hands in delight. "The very thing I need. Harry, you pump some water into that basin, and we'll wash the rhubarb first."

He sprang to do as she said, and she set things up in a row, the basin of water, first. "Harry, you wash the stalks and hand them to Donald." She gave Donald a clean tea towel. "Donald, you dry them and hand them to me." For herself, she set out a cutting board and found a butcher knife. "Then I'll cut them into pieces ready for a pie."

Harry followed her orders. Donald hesitated when Harry handed him a wet stalk until Harry said, "Come on, Donald, there's work to do." The younger boy pulled his fingers from his mouth and dried the stalk.

Irene hid a smile. Such a sober pair. So dependent on each other. "I always like to sing when I work. Don't you?"

Harry's attention on his task, he asked, "Sing what?"

She chopped the rhubarb as she talked. "Anything. We can even make up songs."

Both children stopped working to look at her.

She nodded, her expression serious. "Like this one: Rhubarb, stewbarb. I like rhubarb. It's so tasty. Now let's be hasty and make a rhubarb pie." She sang it in a rolling tune.

Harry chuckled. "Can you make up one about us?"

She thought a moment. "Harry and Donald, oh yeah. Washing and drying, oh yeah. They're a good pair, with nothing they compare. Hurray for Harry and Donald."

Harry grinned.

Donald shot a glance at his older brother, then ducked his head, but not before Irene caught a flash in his dark eyes.

"I can do one for each of you, if you like."

"Okay."

She purposely started with Harry. "There was a young boy named Harry. His looks were as fine as a cherry. He helped out his pa, and oft milked the cow, his work was so fine, oh so very. This young man, I know, more handsome will grow. He makes his dear dad oh-so-merry."

Harry's eyes grew wide and a smile spread across his face. "Sing it again."

She did, loudly, with great gusto until Harry laughed.

She laughed, too, then turned to Donald. "Shall I make up a song about you, Donald?"

He nodded, his expression sober.

"This will have to be a very special song for a special boy." She tipped her head, watching him as she thought about a song. His gaze, dark and intent, never left her face. He was measuring her, assessing her, perhaps wondering if he would allow her to enter into his world. A sobering thought. She prayed she would be found worthy.

"Here goes." She began to sing. "Donald is a little boy, who fills our hearts with joy. His eyes are dark, his hair is, too, I'm glad it's not blue. This little boy is special, see, a little bird told me. His daddy loves him with all his heart, that is quite plain to see."

Donald's gaze never wavered. Irene met it steadily knowing to do otherwise would be to fail him. She finished the song.

Harry chuckled. "Donald, you'd look funny with blue hair."

Irene caught a glimpse of approval in Donald's eyes before he ducked away.

She concentrated on cutting the rhubarb, giving herself a chance to control the way her nose tickled with unshed tears. She couldn't remember being so emotional before.

"I'm done," Harry announced.

"Good job. We'll clean up here, then start pies."

"Can we help?"

"I was counting on it. You dump the water out, then find me a big mixing bowl. Donald, do you think you can find the pie plates?"

The boys scrambled to do her bidding while she wiped the table. When they brought back the requested items, she pressed her finger to her chin. "Either of you know how to make pie crust?"

Two heads wagged back and forth.

"Then we shall begin with a baking lesson. First, we need flour. Here's a cup, Harry. You measure out four cups into this bowl." He carefully did so. "Now we need some lard. Donald, do you know where I could find the lard?"

The little boy stared at her for a moment, his fingers in his mouth.

"Do you know what lard is?"

He nodded.

"I was sure you would. You don't miss much, do you?"

He shook his head.

"Do you know where it is?" When Harry opened his mouth to answer for his little brother, she signaled him to let Donald do it. Harry gave her a quick nod and a little smile that said he understood.

Donald nodded.

"Fine. Will you show me?"

He led the way into the pantry and pointed at a high shelf.

"Hmm. I guess someone didn't know you couldn't reach it up there. I think I'll have to help." She lifted him up so he could reach it, surprised at how little he weighed. She set him down again and took the tin from him, even though she wanted nothing more than to hug this child and assure him he would never be hurt again. "Good job. Now I'll measure the right amount into the flour. Then I need someone to chop it." She looked around the kitchen pretending to look for someone.

"I can help," Harry said.

She dropped her gaze to him. "Why, I do believe you're exactly what I need." She showed Harry how to plunge the pastry blender into the flour, cutting through the lard. He set to the task with a seriousness that touched her heart.

She touched Donald's chin. "And what about this young man? Do you suppose he'd help, too?"

"You want to do this, Donald?" Harry asked, moving over so Donald could climb up beside him. He relinquished the tool to his younger brother, and the pair bent over the bowl.

Irene stood back and watched, her chest so incredibly tight she wondered if she was getting a cold. She let them chop a bit more. "Now I'll add some water and get it ready to roll. Anyone know where the rolling pin is?"

Two boys scrambled from the chair and raced toward the cupboard. Harry let Donald carry it to her.

"Thank you. I don't know how I'd manage without you two. Now comes the fun part." She handed a wad of dough to each boy. "You get to make something, too."

Harry held the dough. "What can I make?"

"Anything you like. You could roll out snowmen shapes. Or you could make a little pie and fill it with jam. Or you could make a braid to bake. Whatever you like."

He nodded, considering. "I'll make a snowman."

"Good choice."

Harry turned to Donald. "You want to make one, too?"

Donald nodded and climbed to a chair beside Harry.

Irene smiled as she fit the bottom crust into the pan. "You know what we forgot to do?"

Two pairs of eyes looked at her.

"We forgot to eat rhubarb raw."

Harry wrinkled his nose. "It's sour."

Irene let her jaw drop, shocked. "You mean you've never learned how to eat raw rhubarb? Well, let me show you."

She poured a little sugar in a cup, picked a piece of the fruit, and dipped it into the sugar. She popped the piece in her mouth and bit down, the sharp and sour making her mouth pucker. Then sweet prevailed. "Umm, good." She pushed the sugar toward the boys. "You try it."

His expression doubtful, Harry dipped a piece into the sugar and popped it into his mouth.

Irene laughed. "You have to bite."

Grimacing, Harry bit down, his first expression startled. He wrinkled his face and chewed furiously. She knew the moment his taste buds acknowledged the sweet.

"Good, isn't it?"

He nodded. "Can I have some more?"

"As much as you want. How about you, Donald?"

He shook his head, his gaze on Harry.

"Come on, Donald. You got to try some." Harry prepared a piece for him. Obediently, Donald opened his mouth, and Harry popped it in. "Now you got to chew real slow."

Donald did so, his expression shocked.

Harry laughed. "It's only sour for a minute. Then it's real good."

Donald finished the piece but could not be persuaded to try another.

The boys returned to patting their dough flat while Irene measured sugar and flour over the fruit, then fit the top crust on.

The pies were in the oven, filling the room with their aroma when the door opened.

Irene glanced up. Zach's face registered shock.

Irene looked about. She had been helping the boys put raisin eyes and noses on their snowmen. Bits of dough lay scattered over the table. A dusting of flour covered the boys' shirts, the table, and even the floor.

"Boys, you're making a mess." His voice deepened with. . .

She didn't know him well enough to understand whether

his displeasure was meant for her for allowing such a mess, or the boys for making it.

She straightened, wiping her hands on a cloth. "It's my fault. I've been showing them how to make pies."

"Look," Harry said. "We've made snowmen. All we have to do is sprinkle them with sugar and bake them." He waited for his father's reaction.

Zach hesitated, then he moved to look over the boys' shoulders. "Dough men," he muttered.

"That's right." Harry nodded vigorously. "They're really dough men, not snowmen. Aren't they nice?"

"Almost good enough to eat."

Irene laughed. "Let's bake them first."

She helped the boys slip them onto a cookie sheet, then slid it into the oven. "I didn't know when to expect you."

He shifted from foot to foot, his troubled glance going from the boys, then back to Irene.

She drew in a deep breath, uncertain what troubled him.

"I'll have dinner ready soon." She'd already thought of a few things she could throw together in a hurry. Fried potatoes from last night, a few scrambled eggs—it wouldn't take long.

"I can wait." He ran a finger along the top of the chair and wiped it on his pants, leaving a white smudge. "I'm sorry the boys made such a mess. I'm sure they didn't mean to."

She laughed. "Boys and kitchens clean up quickly. We were having too much fun to worry about a little flour, weren't we, boys?"

Two little heads bopped up and down. "We learned all about making pies, and she sang us songs—just for us." Harry sounded pleased.

"She did, did she?" His voice carried a note of surprise.

"Sing them for him," Harry begged.

"Oh, I don't know if I can remember them."

"Mine went. . ." And Harry repeated the little song, his voice thin and wobbly. Finished, he fixed his father with a demanding look. "Is that true? Do I make you merry?"

Zach ruffled his hair. "Yes, you do."

"What's merry?"

Irene laughed, meeting Zach's eyes above Harry's head. He grinned crookedly. "It means to be happy and gay."

"That's what I thought. Then I guess it can't be true. You never laugh and play with us anymore."

Zach's expression hardened, and he turned away, taking his time about hanging up his jacket. Finally, he returned to Harry's side. "It won't always be so bad." His dark eyes made Irene want to help him. Touch him.

"That's right," she said. "It will soon be buttons and bows. You wait and see."

Father and son both relaxed at her assurances. Donald let his fingers lay slack in his mouth.

Zach's eyes flashed his thanks. "How long 'til dinner?"

Irene pulled her thoughts together. "Give me half an hour to clean up and fix something." As an afterthought, she added, "You're welcome to sit and have coffee while I work."

"Thanks." He hesitated. "Maybe I will."

She filled the coffeepot with fresh water and ground some more coffee. As she waited for it to boil, she swiped the table clean and ran the broom over the floor.

Zach sent the boys to wash as she sliced potatoes into the frying pan, then checked the oven. "Looks like the dough men are cooked."

The boys hurried to see their creation.

"Careful, it's hot yet." She slid them onto a clean cloth. "We'll let them cool first. That will give us time to eat." She pulled dishes from the cupboard. "Harry, you put on the plates and cups. Donald, you put cutlery at every place."

While the boys set the table, she cracked eggs into the pan. The pies were done, and she set them to cool and dished up the food.

"I'll say the blessing," Zach murmured.

The boys quickly folded their hands and bowed their heads.

"Lord, bless this food. Bless our home with love and peace. Amen."

Tears stung behind Irene's nose. She was certain he didn't know her name meant peace—bringer of peace, but his words made her feel blessed. She took a deep breath and passed the food, helping Donald serve himself an egg.

"How did your morning go?" She handed the plate to Zach.

"Good. I only found a couple places in the fence I had to repair. The grass is coming good."

"You'll have to pardon my ignorance when you talk about the farm. I've never lived on a farm."

"Where did you live?" Harry asked.

"You know I'm from England?"

He nodded.

"That's why I sound funny to you."

"You don't sound funny. You sound nice."

Her heart swelled. "Why, thank you, Harry. That's very sweet."

"I lived with my younger sister and father in a small house in a small town outside London," Irene said. "I loved it when Father took us to London to the shops, and we got to ride the tube. That's the underground rail," she explained for Harry's sake. "My father was an accountant in a small firm."

"Where was your mother?" Harry asked the question, but two little boys waited for the answer.

She knew her answer must be precise in order to let these boys know she understood. "I was eight years old when my baby sister was born. My mother never got strong again. I was ten when she passed away."

The air swelled with the heaviness of her words. She waited, not knowing what each was thinking, but knowing they pushed her words up alongside their own experience to see how it fit.

"Was it your baby sister's fault?" Harry whispered.

"Oh no. My mother loved her very much and wanted to get better, but her body was too weak. Oh no. I can't imagine not having my sister."

"What's her name?" The conversation continued between Harry and Irene, but she sensed Donald's and Zach's keen interest.

"Grace."

"What happened to her?"

"She grew up into a beautiful young girl with golden curls and a sweet smile, and she married your daddy's cousin, Billy Marshall. They live in Toronto. And they are very happy."

Harry sighed. "That's good." He hesitated. "Everybody should be happy."

She felt Zach's surprised start at his son's words, but she kept her attention on Harry, knowing he sought answers for himself. Besides, she was afraid of her own emotions if she looked at Zach. This family—her family, she realized with a jolt of possessiveness—pulled at her heart like it was a ball of yarn to which someone had suddenly given life to some of the strands.

"Yes," she said when she was sure she could speak without her voice cracking. "Everyone should be very happy though maybe not all the time. And sometimes we have to work at it."

"How do you do that?" Harry asked.

"Sometimes we have to really try to find the good things in life rather than letting the bad things swallow us up. Does that make sense?"

He thought about it. "I guess it's a little like eating rhubarb."

She laughed. "It certainly is." She felt Zach's questioning gaze on her and turned to explain. "We ate rhubarb dipped in sugar. The only way to enjoy it is to bite down and let the sour juice mix with the sugar. Then you get a sharp sweetness." She turned back to Harry. "That's a real good way to see it."

The boy's expression remained thoughtful.

Irene jumped up. "Speaking of rhubarb, let's have some of that pie. Do you boys want your dough men, or pie, or both?"

Harry and Donald looked at each other. Then Harry nodded. "We'll have pie now, please, and our dough men later."

Irene chuckled. "Good idea."

Halfway through his piece of pie, Harry turned to Irene again. "Do you still miss her?"

"My mother? Yes, I miss her. I probably always shall. But it doesn't hurt so much anymore."

He nodded and turned back to his pie. "Good pie," he murmured.

"That's because of all the help I had."

"It is good," Zach added. "Thank you."

The boys finished and were excused from the table while Irene and Zach lingered over tea. He rolled his cup back and forth in his hand, his expression thoughtful.

She waited, letting him find his way of saying what was on his mind.

After a few minutes, he shoved his cup away and sighed. "Harry has never said anything about his mother's death. I wasn't here when she. . ." He swallowed. "They sent me word at camp, but by the time I got here. . ." He studied his hands. "Thank you."

"For what?" She was mystified at his meaning.

"For answering his questions."

"I'm glad if I've helped him in some small way."

He rubbed his thumbnail up and down a dark spot on his pant leg. "I don't expect you to do beyond for them."

She stared at the top of his head. Beyond! What *did* the man mean? "Beyond what?"

He straightened then, fixing her with a hard look. "Our agreement was someone to run the house and care for the boys. I'm not expecting you to do beyond that."

Her mouth dropped open. She clamped it shut, knowing she should clamp back the words rushing to her mind, but they burst forth in a torrent. "Are you saying you expect me to cook and clean and tend your boys without enjoying their company? Without answering their questions? Without caring about how they feel? You once said I was crazy, but I'm not the one who is crazy if you think I can live in this house without caring for the people in it, if you think I can function without having feelings." She pushed to her feet. "I'm sorry. No matter what you think our agreement is, I have no intention of pretending I don't have feelings."

She turned her back, busying herself with the dirty dishes,

wishing he would go. She didn't often lose her temper and didn't like it when she did.

His chair pushed back, and she heard him stand. But he didn't leave.

She determinedly kept her back to him.

He sighed loudly. "I'm sorry. I didn't mean it that way."

She waited.

"I just don't want them hurt again."

Drying her hands on a towel, she turned to face him. "Having someone care for them, allowing them to care for me—well, it carries a risk. Caring always does. But to refuse to take that risk—why, to shut love out is the worst hurt of all. 'Tis better to have loved and lost than never to have loved at all.'"

His dark expression told her he wasn't convinced. Without another word, he lifted his coat from the hook and went outside.

She stared after him. She should have bitten her tongue. What right did she have to say anything about loving and losing? She'd never lost a spouse. She knew nothing about how he felt. Yet, as she watched him cross the yard toward the barn, she knew healing would not come until Zach allowed himself to love again. She turned away and plunged her hands into the dishwater. *Don't be a foolish old maid,* she scolded herself. *Love was not part of the bargain.*

But her inner longings would not be quieted despite her mental reminder that Zach was now her husband in a union that was a matter of convenience. She wanted more.

The boys played quietly in the other room while Irene finished the dishes. She reminded herself of her advice to Harry that one sometimes had to work at being happy. *And content,* she added now. She began to hum as she worked.

The door opened, and Zach stood in the doorway. "Where are the boys?"

"Playing in the other room." She wondered if there was something wrong.

"I need Harry to help me fix the plow." He raised his voice. "Harry."

The boys trotted into the room.

"I need you to help me, Harry." He knelt before Donald. "You're needed here to help."

Irene watched the play of emotions across the younger boy's eyes and knew he didn't believe he was being left behind because he was needed. She waited until Zach left. Harry gave Donald a sad look over his shoulder before he followed his father. She faced Donald. "You want to work or play?"

His eager nod answered her.

"Me, too. Why don't you come and see what I brought with me?"

She led the way into the bedroom and knelt before the trunk, waiting for Donald to come to her side. Slowly, she lifted back the lid. On top lay an assortment of books and photo albums. She took a worn book. "This has always been one of my favorite books. It's full of lovely pictures and rhymes." His dark eyes gleamed. "Let's take it into the other room, and I'll read it to you."

Solemnly, he marched to the sofa and climbed up.

Irene sat beside him, careful not to push close enough to threaten him. She opened the book. "See the big fat king?"

Donald's dark head bent over the pages. One finger touched the picture.

"It's Old King Cole." She recited the rhyme, Donald drawing closer, leaning his elbow on her knee as he studied the picture. She read both pages. "Shall we see what's next?"

He shifted enough to allow her to turn the page, then again bent over her knee.

She read on and on, amazed at how this little boy settled against her leg. She dropped her hand to his shoulder. He did not pull away. Next time he shifted for her to turn the page, she drew him into the hollow of her arm. Although he did not snuggle close, neither did he stiffen or pull away.

His little body warmed her, his boy-smell of playing in the hay satisfied her senses. She smiled down at the dark head, her heart drinking in the pleasure of his acceptance.

She turned a page. "Puss in Boots," she murmured.

A sound shuddered through Donald, a sound that stayed inside him. She felt it ripple along his thin ribs and felt certain he had chuckled silently.

"He's a funny kitty, isn't he, with his boots and feathered hat? Can you imagine your kitty acting so silly?"

He touched the picture.

She waited, not reading the story, wondering if he would find a way to indicate whether or not he wanted her to.

He tipped his head toward her, his dark eyes dancing as he tapped the page with his forefinger.

"You want to hear the story about Puss in Boots?"

He nodded once, quite decisively, turned his gaze back to the page, and waited expectantly for her to read.

Irene took a deep breath to ease the tightness in her throat. They came to the end of the book. She closed it.

Donald lifted the cover, demanding more.

"You like my book, do you? Well, I don't blame you. It's always been my favorite, too." Somehow, she felt compelled to talk to this boy, to deepen their connection. He relaxed against her. "I remember my own mommy reading these to me. I never wanted her to stop. Sometimes we sat on the sofa just like this. Sometimes I crawled into bed with her and put my head on her pillow. But you know the very best time of all was when my mama spread a blanket under the trees in our garden and we sat outside with the birds and bees singing as she read."

Donald sprang from her arms and scurried across the room, disappearing into the hall.

"Donald?" She hurried after him and met him coming from his bedroom, a less than clean blanket trailing behind.

Irene chuckled. "Let's do it." She scooped up the blanket. "Lead the way."

Donald marched out the door and headed directly for a grove of trees overlooking the deep valley. The view was intense—giant, snowcapped peaks and the sloping green valley. She spread the blanket. Donald plopped down, looking up at her with a look that plainly asked, *Why so slow?*

She laughed. "Let me look around first. This is such pretty country." She breathed in the murky scent of the farm, the green smell of new leaves on the poplars. She tasted the metallic breeze from off the mountains. She saw the plow, but no sign of Zach or Harry. The barn door stood ajar. They must have gone there.

"I'm ready." She settled beside him. He scooted close, practically curling into her lap. Again she read the book from cover to cover, taking her time, savoring each sensation; memories of her own mother, sweet times of reading to Grace, and now the budding tenderness of this little boy.

The ringing sound of metal against metal jerked her attention toward the plow. Zach and Harry were bent over it, their heads almost touching. Zach's big hands guided the boy's as he concentrated on his task, frowning in concentration.

Zach's deep tones reached Irene. As she listened and watched, her chest tightened. Zach's patience and gentleness with the boys sparked an answering tenderness in her heart. What would it be like to receive the same sort of gentle love? She blinked hard. This was not an arrangement that left room for the usual sort of feelings between a man and his wife. She breathed deeply, promising herself she would be content with small mercies, like this little boy leaning on her knee.

Zach straightened. He lifted his head and saw her sitting under the trees. His eyes widened when he saw Donald at her knee. He stared as if seeing her for the first time.

Distance disappeared as they studied each other. The boys, the mountains—everything disappeared, and there was nothing but Zach and Irene assessing each other, measuring, finding surprises and assessing again.

Her heart pounded in her ears with the insistence of a stubborn knocking at the door. She couldn't remember how to breathe. Inside, she drew toward him, assuring, pleading—for what she didn't know. She only knew she longed for something she didn't understand.

four

That night, Irene again remained in the kitchen while Zach put the boys to bed. She thought of offering to do it, or at least help, but the set of Zach's face as he shepherded the boys to their bedroom made it plain he would not easily share this job. She had no desire to supplant him. She knew the boys would not have allowed it—their love for their father shone like the sun setting over the hoary mountaintops, and she told herself she didn't mind being left out of the nighttime ritual.

She set a copper boiler on the stove and filled it with water for laundry in the morning. She picked up a rag and began wiping the surfaces of the room. Several minutes later, the wet rag hanging in her idle hand, she looked out the window at the glorious display of pinks and reds bursting over the peaks. Harry, serious and sober, seemed to accept her with quiet reservation. Donald allowed her to touch him, almost cuddle him. He warmed to her attempts to get to know him. She felt she had made strides with both boys. It was a satisfying feeling—and an exhilarating one. She'd stepped into a world from which there could be no retreat. She wiped the window ledge and scrubbed fingerprints from the glass.

What would the night bring forth? The time after the boys went to bed remained uncharted territory. She wished there was a way of getting Zach to draw a map of what to expect.

"They're settled in."

She calmed herself before she turned. "They go to bed well."

He shrugged. "They do everything well." He paused. "Perhaps too well."

"Too well? I don't understand."

"Doesn't it strike you as odd that they're a tad too ready to do whatever I say?"

"I hadn't thought about it." She thought about it now, remembering Grace at that age. Her sister hadn't been troublesome, but there were times she exerted her will or made her displeasure known. "I guess I thought they were on their best behavior because they didn't know me."

"No, they never do anything naughty. Sometimes I wish they would. It's like they're only half alive."

"It's been hard on them."

"Yes."

"I'm sure they'll soon be back to normal."

He nodded and gave a half grin. "All buttons and bows?"

"Something like that." His teasing did funny things to the way her heart beat.

He sobered. "I 'spect you're right."

He seemed larger than she remembered, his presence making the room small and warm.

From a shelf to the side of the cupboard, he pulled out a ledger and opened it on the table. "I've got some paperwork to do." He shuffled through a fistful of papers and labored over a row of figures.

She returned to wiping surfaces, removing dark smudges from the wall around the stove and next to the door. Several minutes later, she had circled the room and rinsed out the rag, wiping clean the dishpan as she poured the water down the drain that went outside.

Her neck began to hurt. It wasn't that she'd worked so hard, but everything had been a new experience. A desperate weariness engulfed her.

"Don't bother waiting for me. I'll be a little while sorting this all out."

"If you don't mind, I'll head for bed, then." She turned toward the hall, anger searing through her senses.

He grunted a reply without looking up.

Not until she entered the bedroom did she stop to examine her anger. She thought she'd made it plain this morning that she wouldn't be driving him from his bed. She meant it.

If he didn't understand, then she would be proving it.

She took her time preparing for bed. After she'd crawled under the covers, she opened her Bible and read a few verses. Her heart condemned her. She had no right to be upset about the arrangements. She'd understood them fully when she entered into this marriage. If she were foolish enough to harbor secret longings for something more than a lonely bed and two little boys to smile over, then she had no one but herself to blame for her disappointment.

She prayed for strength and wisdom, then calmed, turned the lantern off, and lay staring at the gray window, ignoring the streak of light from under the door as she listened to the sounds of the house settling for the night. A cow lowed softly. The eerie sound of a coyote's howl shuddered along her spine. Several voices answered the call, bringing a smile to her lips. Even coyotes liked having someone to talk with and share the news of the day. She had lifted the window a crack. The night air was cool, laden with spicy smells. She promised herself she would plant sweet peas beneath the window so she could fall asleep every night to their stirring scent.

The room darkened. Zach had turned out the light in the kitchen. She turned toward the door, listening. The chair scuffed against the floor as he pushed it back. The floorboards sighed as he walked across them toward—she jerked the blankets to her chin and caught her breath in a hard gasp. His steps came toward the bedroom.

She lay stiff, her heart thudding like the beat of the railcar wheels racing along the tracks.

He entered the dark room, making his way around with the measured steps of someone familiar with his surroundings. A lamp stood on the table on his side of the bed, but he made no move to light it. In the darkness, she could see his shadow. His arms lifted, and he shrugged out of his shirt, tossing it over the bedpost. A solid bulk, he stepped out of his trousers.

He didn't move.

She could taste his uncertainty, his dread of this situation. She trembled, suddenly cold.

She sensed his indrawn breath—a gathering of strength as he grabbed the covers on his side and climbed into bed, his weight tipping the mattress toward him. She adjusted her body so she balanced on her side.

He clung to his.

"I thought I would have to find that saw," she muttered.

"No need to be hasty."

She wondered if he meant the saw or their relationship. Either way, his words meant the same. "No. No need to be hasty, but I have certain expectations."

He shuffled about so he was on his back. "Are you having second thoughts, then?"

She stared at the ceiling, a shadow of light from the window making a splash of gray. "I've given my word, and I'll stand by it. My expectations are simply that we make an effort to look like normal married people. I think it's best for the boys."

He grunted agreement. "What about everything else?"

"The farm? The house? You know I've never had any farm experience. But I like what I see. It's a beautiful spot. And you're quite right. We have the best view in the country, if not perhaps in the world. Everything is so neat and tidy. I can tell you take a great deal of pride in this place. The house is small, but it's very cozy. I'm certain it will be warm and tight against the cold. And the boys. . ." She laughed softly. "I don't have to tell you they are the sweetest lads around. I feel we will learn to regard each other fondly." She already felt a fondness that was unfamiliar in its depth. "Listen to me. I do rattle on, don't I?" Embarrassed, she fell silent.

After a moment, he said. "It's okay. Talking is okay."

She smiled into the darkness. Although a man of few words, he had a way of saying things in a concise way she found reassuring. Truth be told, a man who fostered confidence.

His breathing deepened. He rolled toward her. She stiffened as his arm brushed hers, but she dare not move for fear of wakening him. She allowed herself to relax, finding his unconscious touch calming. She smiled into the dark.

Zach was gone when she woke the next morning. Somehow he'd slipped out without disturbing her. So much for her plans to be up early and start the water heating. She dressed hurriedly and dashed from the room. The stove was already hot.

She tested the water. Still cool. She started coffee, then pulled the cumbersome washing machine from the pantry.

The boys came to the doorway.

"As soon as we've had breakfast, I'm going to wash all the dirty clothes." She glanced at the pair. "Anyone know how to do laundry?"

Two heads wagged back and forth.

"Then we shall have lots of fun learning together." A sparkle in Donald's eyes rewarded her.

Harry's gaze rested on the beast of a washing machine. "Aunt Addie said it was a stubborn old machine not fit to live."

Irene laughed. "It looks simple enough." The machine had a large tub for the water, a handle to churn the clothes, and a narrow wringer to wind the clothes through. "Don't you think we can manage it?"

The door behind them opened. "Manage what?"

Irene spun around. "This beast of a washing machine."

"She's going to wash all our clothes," Harry added.

"All the dirty ones," Irene corrected.

A smile slid across Zach's face. "Harry's right. That would be all of them."

She nodded, struck by how the smile softened his features.

"Aunt Addie said the washer was no good." Harry gave it a little kick. "She said if she had a stick of dynamite, she'd blow it up."

Zach raised his eyebrows. "She did, did she?" He circled the machine, his arms crossed over his chest, studying it. "And what exactly did it do to make her say such wicked things?"

Harry solemnly took the handle and pulled on it. It grunted once, then skimmed back and forth without doing anything.

Stepping back, he waited for his father to try it. Zach jerked the handle back and forth. It caught erratically.

"This is easy to fix." He dropped to his knees, adjusted something underneath the machine, and tried it again. It worked fine. "See. Just a loose nut. I'm surprised Addie didn't fix it herself."

"Got to watch out for those loose nuts," Irene muttered.

Zach gaped at her, a slow smile spreading, deepening until he chuckled low in his chest.

The glow inside Irene's chest felt as if she had swallowed the moon.

He sobered. "I feel bad making you do so much work right off the start."

Her smiled dipped a bit at the corners. "I love doing laundry. The steam off the wash water, the smell of soap, hanging out the things, and letting the wind iron them. . . Then all those clean, sweet piles of clothes." She sighed. "It's a satisfying job."

He shook his head. "You sure you don't have a loose nut?"

She laughed so hard the three of them stared at her. "You think I'm crazy because I like work? Did you not say how much you liked work?"

His eyebrows questioned her.

"When I asked you about your likes, you said something about work."

"But I'm a man. Work is what I do."

"A man." She choked. "Seems to me work is what most women do as well. What sort of idea do you have about women and work?"

He turned to look out the window and mumbled, "I thought women preferred other stuff. Like handwork or reading."

"I'm sure we do, but that doesn't mean there's no enjoyment in plain hard work. Like I said, it's satisfying."

He nodded, but she could tell he wasn't convinced.

After breakfast, Irene gathered up mounds of clothes and bedding. She filled the tubs with water.

"Now, I need someone to churn the washing."

"I can." Harry grabbed the handle. "Aunt Addie let me do this before."

"Good. We'll get a system going. Harry, you do that. I'll run them through the wringer. Donald, you get a chair, and you can swish the clothes in the rinse water.

Donald shoved a chair close.

"We'll wait until we're sure these clothes are really clean."

Harry churned the clothes, soap frothing the top of the water.

"Do you think that's good enough?"

Harry nodded.

"Then I'll wring them." She used a long wooden spoon to scoop the articles from the hot water to the wringer, grunting as she turned the handle. "Donald, swirl them around good. We've got to get all the soapy water out." Donald plunged his arms in to his elbows, attacking the clothes with the gusto of a baker kneading dough.

"He's all wet."

"He is, isn't he?" Irene laughed at the pure pleasure on Donald's face. She would have let him walk in the water with his shoes on for a chance to see that look. "But that's easy to fix." She touched the small boy's shoulder. "Wait a minute, Donald." He withdrew sharply as if ashamed of his pleasure. "You're doing a fine job, but it will be more fun if you don't have to worry about your clothes. Let's take them off."

He lifted his arms immediately.

Irene gaped. It was the first time she'd seen him actively cooperate in any aspect of dressing or undressing. Complying quickly, she pulled his shirt off and tossed it into the pile. He put one hand on her shoulder to balance as she removed each shoe and sock, then pulled his legs out of his trousers. "Now you can splash all you want."

He gave her a look as if checking to see if she meant it, then turned back to pumping his arms up and down in the water.

Irene put more clothes in the washer, and Harry pumped the handle back and forth. Irene slipped away one article at a time from the rinse tub and ran it through the wringer, then dropped it into the creaky yellowed basket.

They settled into a comfortable rhythm.

"I think it must be time for a song."

Harry nodded.

Donald kept his attention on his task.

"She'll be coming round the mountain, she'll be coming round the mountain. . ." She sang several verses, then stopped. "I need some help with this song. Harry, you must know it. Sing along."

He gave her a startled look. At first, she thought he would refuse, then as she sang with loud gusto, his quavering thin voice joined hers.

Donald paused, a puzzled look on his face as he studied his brother.

Irene was almost certain she saw the flicker of a smile before Donald turned his attention back to rinsing the clothes.

"What is this?"

Irene broke off in the middle of a verse, so startled by Zach's voice that she almost choked.

"It looks like you're trying to drown each other."

All three of them stood stock-still, Harry with his hands on the handle, Donald with his arms in water, Irene sure her face registered guilt and shock. Water slopped on the floor, dripping from the tubs.

They'd been having such a good time she hadn't given it a thought.

"We're doing the laundry," she announced in a deadpan voice.

"And singing," Harry added, equally serious.

"I noticed. In fact that's why I'm here. I came to see what the racket was all about."

"Racket?" she sputtered. She jammed her hands on her hips, forgetting they dripped. "How do you like that? He calls our singing 'racket.'" She spun on Harry, her lips twitching. "I say, how do you like that?" But she could contain her amusement no longer. She laughed so hard she had to sit down.

Zach shook his head, looking uncertainly at her. "Sometimes I wonder."

"Wonder what?" But she could barely get the words out for the laughter choking her.

He muttered something about a crazy woman.

She sobered enough to say, "It's not crazy to have fun. And we were having a lot of fun. You should hear Harry's 'hee-haw' when she comes round the mountain." She gave Harry a wink. "Best 'hee-haw' I ever heard."

"Look at the mess."

"It's water. Besides, the floor could do with a good scrubbing."

He continued to give her a measuring look. "Most women would have a fit if someone made such a mess."

"I'm guess I'm not most women."

"I guess not."

She squeezed the last pair of trousers through the wringer. "While you're here, you might as well help carry the water out."

He carried the rinse tub out and dumped it down the hill. She watched the water trail down the grassy slope, wishing there was a rosebush there to enjoy the moisture.

He drained the washer for her and dumped the water while she hung the clothes, filling the lines. She stepped back, enjoying the way the clothes billowed in the breeze and turned to see Zach watching her with a puzzled look on his face.

She laughed. "Maybe I'm a bit daft, but I do like to see lines full of clean laundry."

He continued to stare.

"It's not a crime, you know."

He smiled tightly. "I guess not."

She snorted. "One would think you'd prefer me to sit and moan about all the work rather than taking pleasure in it."

"I'm not sure what I want."

"That's a fact." She recalled Addie's words: *"Even Zach doesn't know what Zach wants."* "Thanks for emptying the tubs."

He nodded. "Guess I better get back to work. I want to get to the fields by Monday."

"And I'd like to get the floor cleaned up before someone comes in and complains about the mess." She gave him a cheeky grin.

His smile was lopsided, his expression uncertain. "I wasn't complaining." He hesitated. She knew he wanted to say more and waited.

"I was thinking you would be upset at the boys for making a mess."

She touched his arm, wanting nothing more than to chase away his endless worry about the boys. "Zach, if this is going to work, you need to get one thing straight in your mind." She waited until his dark eyes met hers. "Our marriage included being a mother to these boys. Now I will perhaps never love them as much as their own mother did, but I care about them with my whole heart. I will never intentionally do anything to hurt them. Indeed, I will do whatever lies within my power to see that they have a good and happy life."

She waited as he contemplated her words.

Finally, he nodded. "I know that. You've already proved it."

Pleased at his acknowledgment, she smiled. "Thank you. You don't know how much that means to me."

His dark gaze drew her in, letting her venture close to his heart, then he jerked away. "I best be getting back to work."

Her thoughts unsettled by his lightning-quick changes, she hurried back to the kitchen.

She found clean, albeit too small, clothes for Donald. "Now, I want you two to go play outside while I clean up the floor."

Donald took Harry's hand.

"What things do you like to do outside?"

"We could go see the kittens."

"Your father would approve?"

Harry nodded. "As long as there are no animals in the barn, we may go out there."

"Good." She had been about to remind Harry to watch his

little brother but stopped herself. The warning was as unnecessary as reminding the sun to rise in the east.

As she scrubbed the floor, her thoughts circled on the strangeness of her situation—married to a man who was not only a stranger, but one who had made it clear he didn't need a wife as much as he needed a permanent housekeeper and substitute mother for his boys. She smiled as she thought of the boys. Already they had found their way into her heart and were winding themselves around it. Caring for and loving them—caring for the house and taking pleasure in her work should be enough to satisfy anyone.

She sat back on her heels, pushing the hair from her face, and wondered if it would be enough for her. There was something about Zach that made her long for more. Her cheeks burned as her imagination suddenly landed in the bedroom with Zach beside her in the bed. She ached to be held in his arms.

She hurried outside to dump the water, acknowledging her need—a need that would not be met. Yet it was better than being an old maid. And she could think of no place she'd rather be.

After dinner, Zach said, "I'll be riding over to see the Millers about getting seed wheat."

Harry surged forward.

"There's no need for you to go, Son. You stay home and have fun with Donald and your new mama."

Irene shot Zach a grateful look, knowing he had acknowledged his trust in her.

Harry opened his mouth to argue, sat back, and nodded. "I 'spect she'll need my help."

Zach met Irene's gaze above the child's head. Neither smiled, but something akin to shared joy passed between them. "I'm sure you're right."

Zach paused before he left. "I'll be back for supper."

"Thank you."

After he left, she studied the boys.

They waited with sharp-eyed interest.

"I can think of a lot of things I need help with, but of course, first we have to clean up the dinner dishes."

Harry sprang up. "I can help." He carried his dishes to the counter where hot, soapy dishwater waited.

Nodding, Donald followed his big brother's example.

She washed, letting Donald dip the dishes in clear water to rinse them. Harry dried. And as they worked, she sang.

"There. That didn't take long." She wiped the basin and took the towel from Harry and hung it to dry.

They waited.

"How about we do a surprise for your dad?"

Two heads nodded.

"Let's clean all the weeds from the garden."

Harry looked doubtful.

"I think we should pile them up, then when your daddy comes home, maybe he'll burn them. Wouldn't it be fun to have a big bonfire?"

One little boy smiled; the other looked pleased, his dark eyes gleaming.

Out in the garden, she surveyed the ruin.

"Lots of weeds," Harry commented.

"Yes, but we can do this if we work together." She showed them how to break the stalks at the ground. Their piles at each end grew steadily.

Irene talked as she worked. "When I was a little girl back in England, we had a little kitchen garden out back. A kitchen garden," she explained, "is where we grew the vegetables and herbs we used in the house. It was a small garden," she continued, "but I loved it. All the neat little rows   All the fresh little plants pushing upward. . . Father grew lovely roses in the rose garden. He could never understand how I preferred the kitchen garden to his rose garden. Not that I didn't like the roses. I did."

She grunted as she pulled a tough stalk. "He didn't understand how I like sturdy, practical things. I liked the idea of something being useful." She surveyed their work. The bulk of the dried plants had been wrested from the ground. The soil looked rich and productive. "This is a lovely, big spot for a garden."

"What will you grow?" Harry asked.

"Vegetables. Tons of vegetables. Rutabagas, parsnips, string beans, squash, onions, greens, and potatoes. And flowers." She pointed to the bedroom window. "I'm going to plant sweet peas under the bedroom window so I can smell them every night when I go to sleep. And I'll plant rows of marigolds and chrysanthemums."

She grinned down at the two little faces regarding her with open mouths. "We'll eat like kings and queens. We'll dine on the finest of food. And we shall be very happy." She grabbed the boys' hands and danced around in a circle, their feet scuffing the dried leaves into powdery dust. "Happy, happy, happy. We'll be as happy as can be," she sang as they danced round and round.

Determined to prove she wasn't quite crazy, she had the boys washed and dressed in clean clothes when Zach came home. The laundry had been folded, some set aside to iron, and a full meal waited to be served.

Irene heard the wagon approaching. She checked her reflection in the picture hanging by the pantry. She paid scant attention to the lush English garden beneath the glass, seeking only to assure herself that her hair lay tidy. Her brown hair looked red and green and pink, reflecting back the colors of the garden but she could see the outline well enough to determine she was tidy. In the silver foil edging of the picture, she caught the sight of her eyes, their light brown turned to gray in the silver reflection. She sighed. No point in trying to fool oneself. She had always been plain. All she could aim for now was tidy. Satisfied, she turned away and hustled the boys outside.

By the time Zach came back from the barn, the three of them waited in a line. Irene checked the boys out of the corner of her eye. They were spotless, straight as soldiers, joined as always by their clasped hands.

Zach ground to a halt.

"Welcome home, Mr. Marshall." She curtsied demurely, keeping her eyes down with what she hoped was the right amount of modesty.

"Hi, Dad," Harry said. "She said we should give you a proper welcome to make up for the mess the last couple times you've come in."

Irene moaned. "You weren't supposed to tell him that. You were supposed to let him think we could always be like this."

"I was? We can?" Harry sounded so deflated that Irene laughed.

"We could try. I think your father would like that." She met Zach's look then, his expression both bemused and bewildered.

"Could we just do things halfway?" he murmured.

"Halfway what?"

"Forget it. I'm beginning to think you wouldn't know what I mean."

She tossed her head back in an airy fashion. "You're quite right. I don't intend to live life halfway."

"Forget it," he muttered. "Only the word 'sedate' springs to mind."

She curtsied again. "But sir, how much more sedate could I be?"

He relented and grinned. "I think it must have to start on the inside to be truly effective."

Harry pushed close to his father. "What's sedate?"

Zach gave Irene a long, steady look. "Something I think we have seen the last of."

For a heartbeat—a very long, hard, heartbeat—Irene and Zach took stock of each other. Irene, wanting to please, yet only knowing her way of doing things, tried to determine if Zach was truly displeased with her or only feeling a little unsettled by her behavior. But she could not tell what he was thinking. All she knew was his dark, steady gaze had a very unsettling affect on her. Her cheeks grew warm. A tiny pulse beneath her jaw beat with totally unfamiliar strength.

She turned away, her bearing upright and steady, her emotions under firm control. "Your meal awaits you, kind sir." She didn't wait to see if he followed but walked slowly to the house, her steps firm and measured. She had lied to him. She'd said she didn't intend to live life halfway, but that's exactly what she was doing. She was half a wife with a heart that didn't know what it wanted.

Over supper, Zach turned to the boys and asked, "What did you do all afternoon?"

Donald turned to Harry. "We cleaned out the garden," said the older boy.

Zach dropped his hand to the table. "You what?"

"Yup," Harry nodded. "We piled up all the weeds. She says you would let us burn it. We could have a big bonfire."

Irene's heart sank at the dark look on Zach's face. "I said maybe you'd let them have a fire."

His expression did not soften. "I told you I would get to the garden."

She stared. "Was I to understand that I was forbidden to do it?"

"You were not forbidden. But you didn't need to do it. I would have gotten it cleaned up in plenty of time." His voice was hard.

She bowed her head, praying for wisdom. After a second, she lifted her head and faced him squarely. "I'm not sure I know what the problem is. Is it that I did the work? Or that I've made you feel guilty?" She rushed on before he could answer. "You need to make clear what things you don't want me tampering with. I don't know the rules if you don't tell me." She filled her lungs and hurried on. "If I've made you feel guilty for some reason, I didn't intend to. I liked working in the garden. I think the boys enjoyed helping me." She held up her hands helplessly. "I don't understand."

"Dad. We had fun." Harry's voice thinned with strain.

Irene shot Zach a pleading look. He quickly sat back. "Don't worry, Son. I'm not angry. I'm glad you had a good afternoon."

Harry relaxed.

Zach shot Irene a dark glance, making it plain they would finish their discussion later.

five

Zach and the boys burned the piles of weeds while Irene cleaned the kitchen. She welcomed the chance to be alone and sort out her feelings. She didn't understand Zach's attitude toward her work. Had she inadvertently done something he disapproved of? But what could it be? She prayed for wisdom to understand the situation.

Zach brought the boys in and supervised their washing up, then took them to the bedroom to get them ready for bed.

Irene made tea to fortify her for the discussion that lay ahead.

"Can I get you a cup?" she asked when he returned to the kitchen. At his nod, she poured tea and set it before him, then sat across the table, clutching her own cup.

He spooned sugar into his tea and stirred it until Irene feared he would wear a hole in the bottom of the cup.

After a few minutes, when he still hadn't spoken, she cleared her throat.

Zach's glance jerked toward her, then returned to his tea.

She took a deep breath and began. "I think we need to talk."

"I suppose." He shifted back in his chair, still intent on stirring his tea.

"Would you explain why you're upset about me cleaning the weeds from the garden?"

He fixed her with a dark look for a second before he answered. "It doesn't seem right."

Irene shrugged. "Do you mean it is unladylike? Unseemly? Or too hard?" She shook her head. "I'm afraid I don't understand."

"It's too much." His gaze rested somewhere beyond her head.

She wiped the rim of her cup. His answers made her head swim. "Too much what?"

He tapped his spoon on the rim of the cup and set it on the

table, then turned his cup round and round. "Too much work."

A suspicion sprouted in her thoughts. She prayed for wisdom. "Zach, I know nothing about your first wife, but I get the distinct impression I do things much differently than she did."

He watched her with a keenness that made her want to look away, but knowing this was an issue that had to be resolved, she clenched her hands more tightly around her cup and kept her gaze steady.

"I feel like you're having a hard time accepting that." She took a deep breath. "But I cannot take her place. I cannot be her substitute, taking over where she left off, doing things exactly the same way. I'm a different person as you're discovering. I quite likely enjoy different things. I will certainly make mistakes and get muddled at times, but it's the only way I can be. I can only be me. Not her."

"I know." The sad resignation in his voice stung.

"Surely it's not that bad."

He didn't answer at first.

"It's not bad," he said finally, sounding surprised by his own decision. "Only a little like coming unseated from the saddle."

"That sounds downright dangerous."

His gaze sought hers, gleaming with some dark emotion she couldn't identify; then his gaze slid past her to stare out the window.

She drew a breath past the sudden tightness in her throat.

Peace settled around them, colored by the flaming painting of the sky. Irene sighed. "It's so very beautiful."

"Worth getting out of bed for, all right."

Her cup rattled in the saucer. Bed. That unknown factor in their relationship.

He turned toward her and gave a thin smile. "You worked hard today. I 'spect you're tired."

It would be impossible to deny as she struggled to smother a yawn. "I guess I am."

"Go ahead. I'll be along later."

She set her cup and saucer on the counter and made her way to the bedroom.

"Thank You, God," she whispered as she lay reading her Bible. It had been a good day. She'd had a good time with the boys and felt she'd crossed another bridge in her relationship with Zach.

She waited for Zach. Minutes passed, and he didn't come. The erratic beat of her heart calmed. Finally, she turned off the lantern. Only after the light was gone did she hear him cross the kitchen and enter the bedroom. Again, he undressed in the darkness and crawled into bed, clinging to his side. "Good night," he murmured.

"Good night," she replied.

❧

Irene set a pot of stew to simmer, then stepped into the parlor. Front room, she reminded herself.

"Harry, Donald, let's go for a walk."

The boys jumped up from their blocks, pausing to look behind them as the tower tumbled and blocks bounced along the floor. Two little heads turned to see her reaction.

"We'll pick them up when we come back. It's too nice a day to spend indoors."

"Where are we going?" Harry asked.

"Do you have a favorite place?"

Donald and Harry exchanged looks. "We aren't allowed to go past the corral fence."

"Then we'll explore together. Let's go down the road." She waved the boys through the door. They ran outside, then stopped, waiting for her.

"Who wants to race?"

Harry jumped up and down. "I do." Donald tugged his hand. "We do."

Irene looked around. Zach had gone to a field to pick rocks; she couldn't see him. A little foolishness would go unnoticed. "See that corner post?" She pointed toward the fence.

Harry nodded.

"I'll race you to that."

He gave her a doubtful look. "You're bigger."

She laughed. "You're probably faster, but to make it fair, I'll let you have a head start."

He nodded and pulled Donald to face the right direction.

"On your mark," she began.

Harry leaned forward, Donald imitating his stance.

She hugged a smile to herself at their intensity.

"Get set. Go."

Two little boys raced toward the fence.

She counted to five. "Here I come!"

"Hurry, Donald!" Harry yelled. "Hurry! We gotta beat her."

Pleasure swelled from deep inside her, erupting in great shouts of laughter, making it almost impossible for her to run.

Harry reached the post, half dragging Donald after him. "We won! We won!"

Irene bent over, breathless from trying to run and laugh at the same time. "You sure did." She collapsed on the ground. "You two can really run, can't you?"

He nodded shyly and plunked down beside her. Donald edged his way in between them.

"You two lads are a lot of fun. I don't know when I've laughed so hard." It was a sobering thought. Life had grown so serious during the war. She flung herself on her back. "Look at all those clouds. Look, do you see that big fish?"

The boys tipped their heads skyward. "Where?" Harry asked.

"Up there." She pointed. "Lay on your backs so you can see better."

Donald's warm body pressed against her side.

Harry pointed. "There it is. I see it. Now it's a ship."

"What do you see, Donald?" she asked.

He sucked the fingers of his other hand and kept pointing.

"It's a cow," Irene said.

"No," Harry said. "It's a bird." And when he laughed, Irene did, too. It was so good to enjoy life with these two.

She jumped to her feet, pulling the boys after her. "Come

on, lazybones. We won't get anywhere lying around here."

Marching together, Harry and Irene singing, they headed down the road, pausing to examine every rock and flower and bush. By the time they arrived back at the house, Harry's pockets bulged with rocks, and Irene's hands were filled with flowers.

"I'll put these in water and be right back." She left the boys on the step while she dashed in and filled a jug with water. She brought cookies and milk out for the boys.

They sat in companionable silence, munching on cookies and sipping milk.

Idly, Irene picked up a rock and tossed it. It clattered a few feet from them.

Harry reached down, picked up another rock, and threw it. "Mine went farther," he said as it bounced on the ground.

Irene selected another with great care and threw it harder. It bounced across the path. "Mine went farther."

Harry picked up a handful of rocks, stood to his feet, and pitched a rock. It zinged through the air, landing several yards away. "Farther," he announced with satisfaction and sat down again.

Irene grabbed a rock, stood, and winged one with all her might. She waited to see where it dropped, then dusted her hand on her skirt. "Farther." She sat down and grinned smugly.

Harry stood again. He angled his body to one side and wound up like a professional and let it fly. It landed close to the spot where her last rock lay. "Farther." He stood over her belligerently.

"I don't think so."

"Wanna bet?"

"I'm sure your father would be shocked to hear you wanting to bet."

"Guess so," he muttered.

"Besides, throwing rocks doesn't take any skill. Not like hitting something."

"Like what?"

She grinned. "Get a tin can and set it over there on that rock." She pointed to a flat rock about twenty feet away.

As Harry hurried to find a can, Irene grinned down at Donald. "You want to try?"

He shook his head, sucking hard on his fingers.

"Here, see how far you can throw." She handed him a small stone.

He took it, clenching it in his fingers, his eyes studying her. Without looking, he tossed it.

"Not bad. But not good enough for a big boy like you." She handed him another. "Try again."

This time he looked at his stone, then toward the grass where Harry and Irene had been throwing their rocks. He lifted his hand over his head and threw the stone. It landed three feet away.

"Way to go!"

He reached out, picked up another stone, and threw it, turning to her for approval.

She squeezed his arm. "You've got a good arm for throwing. Here's Harry back with a tin can. You can take turns, too, if you like."

Harry set the can on the rock and returned to Irene's side.

"Only small rocks," he ordered as he filled his hands.

"Fine with me." She selected a handful and stood at his side. "Donald wants a turn, too." She waited for the younger boy to pick up some rocks. "You go first, Donald."

He stood up and threw his rock. It landed short of the tin.

"Good try." She turned to Harry. "Who's first, you or me?"

"You're oldest. You have to go last."

"Go ahead, then."

He pitched. The stone fell to the right of the tin.

"Too bad," she murmured. "My turn." Her rock fell closer but was still wide of the mark.

Harry took another turn, then Irene. Donald sat down, content to watch. Neither came close to the mark. Soon they didn't bother with turns, they simply kept throwing.

"Who keeps moving the tin?" Irene asked, then threw a handful of rocks.

Harry did the same, taking a step closer.

Irene grabbed another handful and stepped closer.

Harry took two steps.

Irene followed.

Soon they were running toward the tin, pelting rocks as they ran. They were a few feet from it before the tin clattered to the ground as their missiles finally made contact.

"Yay!" Irene cheered.

Harry jumped up and down, yelling.

"What's all the noise?" Zach asked.

Harry's arms dropped to his sides as Irene's heart descended abruptly.

"We're throwing rocks," Harry announced.

"Really? And why would that be?" He stood beside Donald, his arms crossed over his chest.

"Target practice." Irene faced him squarely.

"And all the screaming?"

She drew herself up tall. "We weren't screaming. We were cheering."

"Hit the target." Harry was as serious as she, and she shot him a grateful look.

"The tin can being the target, I gather?"

"Don't be so superior." She marched toward him. "Target practice is important."

"Certainly. Can't argue that. Never know when you might have to defend yourself from empty tin cans." He chuckled.

"Quite so." She paused in front of him.

"I certainly am glad to see you teaching these boys to defend themselves."

She grinned. "It's a job, and somebody's got to do it." His answering smile stirred her senses like a soft spring day.

"So who won the throwing contest?" His gaze held Irene in a gentle grasp. She couldn't look away.

"I did," Harry announced.

"No, you didn't." She sounded out of breath, and she forced herself to breathe slowly. "It was a draw."

"I'm going to practice," the boy said and, picking up more rocks, began to aim them at the tin.

Irene edged past Zach. "Are you here for supper or just to see what all the racket is about?"

"Could be both."

She nodded. "The meal is ready. I put stew on before we went out to pla—" She caught herself. "Walk," she corrected.

Behind her Zach's chuckle rumbled in his chest. "Come on, Donald." He scooped up the child. "I think we should get washed up." He called Harry to come in.

Later, after the supper dishes were cleaned up, she joined Zach in the front room where he sat reading a farm magazine. The boys played with their toys, but as soon as she sat down, they looked at her as if they had a plan.

She leaned toward them. "What do you two have up your sleeves?"

Before he answered, Harry smiled at Donald. "Will you play hide-and-seek with us?"

She'd played the game with them several times, enjoying it as much as they. They'd played it indoors, in the trees, and in the barn.

"I'd like that. I'll go to the kitchen and count to twenty while you and Donald hide." She paused before she stepped from the room. "Now don't make it too easy for me."

His eyes narrowed, Zach lowered his magazine and watched her hurry out.

She counted out loud. "Eighteen. . .nineteen. . .twenty!" she called. "Here I come. Ready or not." She stepped into the room. "Now where could those two be?"

Zach kept his head bent studiously over his magazine.

"I see I'll get no help from you," she muttered.

"I'm minding my own business."

She planted her hands on her hips and spoke to the room in general. "Last time Donald hid behind the sofa." She leaned over. "Not there." She surveyed the room. "I'll guess he's. . ." Her voice dropped to a whisper. "I think I see a little pair of feet." Down on her hands and knees, she crept behind Zach's chair. Donald's big brown eyes stood out round as plates. "Aha! I found you!" And she grabbed him, mock wrestled him to the floor, and tickled him. He squirmed like a playful puppy.

Their play rolled them into the side of Zach's chair. Reaching down to steady them, he grabbed Irene's shoulder. "Careful there," he muttered.

She stopped like she'd slammed into a wall. His touch burned through her skin into a place somewhere behind her heart. A place unfamiliar, untried. She gulped and jerked to her feet, pulling Donald with her, pushing away the enticing invitation from that unfamiliar place.

"Where do you think we'll find Harry?"

Donald's eyes gleamed, but he regarded her solemnly, refusing to give away his brother's hiding place.

"Let's see." She pretended to concentrate very hard when in reality there were only a few places where one could hide. "He's not behind the sofa." She looked hard at Donald. "He wasn't with you, was he?"

Donald shook his head.

"I guess I'll have to look for him, won't I?"

Donald nodded once.

Holding Donald by the hand, she edged along the front of the sofa. "Be very quiet," she whispered to the little boy, "so we can sneak up on him." She tiptoed to the end of the sofa, pressing her finger to her lips to warn Donald not to make a sound. She bent over and peered around the corner. "Boo!"

But Harry wasn't there. She gaped at Donald who bounced with amusement. "Where did he go?"

Again she peaked behind the sofa. "He's not there. Ahh. He's tricked me. But not for long." She edged silently back the length of the sofa, pausing at the arm. "Ready?" she whispered quietly to Donald.

He nodded, his eyes sparkling.

She leaned around the end table.

Harry leapt at her. "Boo!" he shouted, launching into her.

She let his small body bowl her over, pulling Donald to the floor with her, catching Harry in her arms as she rolled.

They came to a halt jammed against Zach's feet.

He lowered his magazine and looked at them. "You're all tangled up like old wire." He lifted Donald off Irene as Harry scrambled to his feet. Then Zach held out a hand to Irene. She grabbed it and jerked to her feet, heat burning up her neck.

Zach held her hand even after she'd regained her feet. Her mind swirled with errant thoughts as he held her gaze. For a moment, only she and Zach existed, the little boys forgotten as his steady, dark eyes pulled her closer and closer.

Harry flung himself on the sofa chortling. "I scared ya, huh?"

She pulled herself together, withdrawing her hand. For a moment, she pressed it to her middle, then ruffled Harry's hair. "You certainly did." She grabbed Donald, pulling him to her lap and laughing like her thoughts weren't tumbling over themselves, sat beside Harry. "You bowled me right over."

Harry nodded, pleased with himself.

Irene sobered. "But I think we should play something quiet now. Donald, why don't you choose a book to read?"

He jumped from her lap and went to the narrow table where she had stacked some of her own books. When he chose the one she had told him was her favorite, her throat tightened. He climbed up beside her. Both boys leaned over her knees as she read.

She felt Zach's gaze on her and glanced up, having no need to look at the page. His expression was thoughtful. She faltered on the familiar words and mustering her well-developed self-control, turned her attention back to the book on her lap.

That night, as they lay in bed in the darkness, eight inches of strangeness between them, Zach said, "Tomorrow's Saturday. I thought I should tell you so you can be ready for church Sunday."

She contemplated his words for a minute, then turned on her

side. "What will people think when you come in with me?"

A sound rumbled from him. "I 'spect they'll think you're a very lucky woman."

She chortled at his bold self-assurance. "I suppose you're right. Am I in any danger from thwarted young ladies or their mothers?"

"It will no doubt be a full-time job for me and the boys to protect you."

Hearing the amusement in his serious words, she laughed. "Perhaps our target practice will come to good use."

The sound of laughter in his voice strengthened. "I hope we don't have to resort to throwing rocks."

But despite the joking, Irene lay staring into the darkness, a trickle of uncertainty making her muscles tense. After a few minutes, she sighed. "I suppose the worst they could do is run me out of town."

His deep voice, very close to her ear, rumbled with sleepiness. "Why would they do that? You've done nothing immoral." He paused. "At least not in marrying me."

"I know. But people have a way of interpreting things."

"I wouldn't worry if I were you. Between the war and the flu epidemic, many families have found themselves doing things they wouldn't have thought of under normal circumstances. Death makes us all equal."

"You're right, of course." Her fears calmed by his words, she squirmed around seeking a more comfortable position.

"Lie still," his sleepy voice commanded.

She obeyed, his deep voice sifting through her. Instantly, she was asleep.

❧

"Tomorrow is Sunday," she said to the boys as she filled the kettle and set it to boil. "We have to get ready. Everyone needs to wash their hair." She squinted at them. "And I think have it cut." She fingered the scissors she'd located in the pantry.

Harry touched his hair. "You're going to cut it?"

She laughed at his apprehension. "Didn't I tell you I

worked in a hospital where we cared for injured soldiers?"

He leaned forward, his hair forgotten. "You did? Solders? Did you see air pilots?"

"I certainly did. In fact, that's where Grace met Billy, your father's cousin. He had been shot in the leg."

Harry's eyes grew round.

"He needed to rest for it to get better." She snorted. "Not that Billy let it rest much. He was forever getting out of bed when he'd been ordered to lie still. Amazing his leg healed so well."

"Did you see airplanes?"

"Lots of them." For the first time it hit her how removed from the war this part of the world had been. Thankfully, these little boys had been spared that horror. Losing a parent was more than enough for them to contend with. "Sometimes those soldier boys needed a haircut. I cut many a head of hair." She set up basins and towels on the table as she talked. "Of course, they were soldiers. They weren't afraid."

Harry drew himself up and squared his shoulders. "I'm not afraid."

"I'm glad to hear it. Now jump up here, and I'll wash your hair; then you can sit outside, and I'll cut it."

He marched forward to obey.

A few minutes later, she toweled his hair dry. "Your turn, Donald."

Donald climbed up on a chair and obediently tipped his head over the basin for her. "Good man," she murmured and quickly scrubbed and toweled his head.

A clean towel in hand, she carried a chair outdoors. "Harry, you're first."

He sat squarely on the chair, allowing her to tuck a towel around his shoulders. "Are you going to cut it just like a soldier's?"

"Of course." Truth be told, she knew only one hairstyle. It had suited the soldiers; it would suit the boys. She bent over her task, nipping Harry's hair short. A few minutes later, she straightened. Standing in front of Harry, she tipped her head from side to side, surveying the results. "All buttons and bows you are." She whipped the towel from his shoulders.

Harry ran his hands over his head. "I'm a soldier now." He bounced from the chair.

Irene turned to Donald. "Your turn, young man."

He climbed up without hesitation.

She wondered how she would disengage his fingers from his mouth, but when she held the towel up to wrap around his shoulders, he folded his hands together in his lap. "Good boy," she murmured, pleased at his cooperation.

He sat still as a rock as his dark locks joined his brother's.

"All done." She lifted the towel, shaking the hair into the wind. "Maybe a bird will build a nest with your hair."

"Do they do that?" Harry asked.

"That's what I was told." She chuckled. "I guess you'd call it a *Harry* nest."

Harry looked pleased at the idea; then the double meaning of the words hit him, and he laughed out loud, a thin, musical sound that reminded Irene of cheery birds.

Irene chuckled as she went inside to wash her hair.

She took the pins out and finger combed her hair before she bent over the basin and poured water over her head. Her long hair took more water and more scrubbing than the boys' hair had. By the time she finished, water trailed down her cheeks and dripped off her nose. She squeezed the water from her hair and blindly reached for the towel, patting the table in an effort to locate where she'd laid it.

"Here," Zach said, his large hand pressing it to her fingers.

"Thanks," she murmured from behind the curtain of hair, as if it were quite normal for a man to observe her at this task. She used the time it took to wrap the towel around her head to settle the sudden lurch of her emotions. When she finally turned to face him, calmness had returned. "We're getting ready for Sunday," she said quite unnecessarily.

"I see the boys have been shorn." He grinned, his eyes dark with mystery.

"I hope you don't mind."

"Of course not. It's an improvement." He ran his big hand over his own hair. "I suppose I could take a pruning as well."

She snorted. "Pruning, indeed. You make it sound quite dreadful." She grinned to show she wasn't offended. "Are you asking me to cut your hair?"

His eyes sparkled. "Would you mind?"

Tipping her head to study him, she admitted his hair hung long around the ears and neck. "I don't mind but let me brush and dry my hair first."

"No rush." He remained in the middle of the floor, arms crossed over his chest, watching her as she poured the basin of water down the drain.

She hesitated, confused by the expression on his face. "I was planning to sit outside to dry my hair." She edged toward the door.

"Go ahead." He followed, dragging a chair with him, tipping it back on two legs.

She hurried to the other chair, her thoughts tripping over themselves. His presence as she toweled her hair and attacked the knots with her brush unsettled her in a way she couldn't explain. Why should she feel so on edge with him? After all, she'd slept beside him several nights without this sudden tingling of her nerves. Aware of his dark eyes watching her, Irene gave her hair more concentration than normal.

"It's a fine day."

Zach's words, so ordinary, calmed her jitters.

She lifted her face to the sun, letting the warm breeze sift through her hair. "It's lovely." She filled her nostrils with the scent of pines and musky earth. "Too bad we couldn't bottle this smell. We could sell it around the world. We'd be rich as kings." She smiled at him, but at the look in his eyes, her smile froze.

"I wouldn't trade places with a king." His voice held a husky note. His eyes, steady and warm, sent a rush of warmth to her heart.

"Are you ready to cut my hair?"

Calling to all the self-discipline she had mastered through the years, she shook her hair over her shoulders. "As soon as I pin my hair up."

"Leave it." His words sounded strained.

"I beg your pardon."

"Leave it down." He cleared his throat. "It will dry better."

She tried to think of something to say. She opened her mouth to speak, but nothing came out. Her heart thundered so loud she wondered if he could hear it. She jumped to her feet. "I'll get the scissors."

She paused inside the door and took a shaky breath. *Steady, old girl,* she warned herself. Her movements sure and firm, she grabbed the scissors and returned outdoors.

Zach sat with the towel around his shoulders, the edges barely covering the bulk of his crossed arms.

She hesitated but a heartbeat, then stepped to his side. "Anything special?" she asked.

He considered her out of the corner of his eye. "All I ask is you do your best."

"Fine." She giggled. "All my haircuts are the same."

He nodded. "Didn't I guess that?"

Her senses assailed by the salty, warm scent of him, she leaned closer. She had never had a chance to study him so close. From this vantage point, she could see a tiny scar traversing his nose. Although he shaved every day, he had a dark shadow that emphasized his squarish jaw.

Her hand was steady as a rock, surprising, she thought, when her insides quaked like rubber as she slid her fingers through his hair to lift the strands. *Stop being a silly old maid,* she scolded herself. Why should she react so strongly to his nearness? After all, it wasn't like she hadn't touched other men in her duties as a nurse.

She tightened her lips. She wasn't a nurse here. She was a wife. Wife. The very word carried the right of intimacy. She swallowed hard and snipped a bit from the ends of his hair. Intimacy, she reminded herself, that she had given up all right to when she'd agreed with Zach's conditions of this marriage.

Having settled the issue in her mind, she relaxed.

"Don't move," Zach murmured.

She froze. "What's the matter?"

"Turn around slowly and look down the valley."

She did as he said. Two deer tiptoed across the bottom of the valley.

"Boys," Zach whispered hoarsely to the two playing nearby. "Look. Quiet now."

They obeyed. Harry whispered, "Oh"—a sound round with awe.

The creatures slid into the shadows of some trees and disappeared.

"How beautiful," Irene whispered as she turned and smiled at Zach.

"Yes," he murmured. "I wouldn't trade places with a king." He held her in his gaze.

She returned to the haircut, her thoughts settled. She hadn't given up anything, she reminded herself, set as she was to being an old maid. Look what she'd gained. "I quite agree. I'm privileged beyond imagination to be here." Let him take that any way he wished.

But he remained silent.

six

Zach pulled the buggy in beside an assortment of vehicles; two shiny black automobiles, one longer, slicker auto, several wagons, a variety of buggies, and a row of horses.

"Looks like I'll have to face the entire community," Irene muttered.

Zach shot her a sharp look. "It's church. Not a public hanging."

She remained doubtful. "I hope you're right."

"I'm always right." His smug confidence made her laugh.

"Much better," he murmured close to her ear as he lifted her down to stand beside him. "I've gotten used to seeing your smile."

She cocked her head at him. "I thought you found me a bit too silly."

"Never said anything of the sort." He held out his arm.

Irene tucked her hand around his elbow, and he pressed it close to his side. He took Harry's hand; she reached for Donald, pleased when he took his fingers from his mouth and readily took her hand. The sticky moisture in her palm didn't bother her a bit.

"Let's face your executioners," Zach said, his tone serious.

"United we stand." She lifted her chin and marched beside him to the door. Several heads turned. At least three women whispered behind their hands as they passed. Irene set her face forward and refused to pay attention.

"You're here. I'm so glad to see you again." Etta, the preacher's wife, bounced down the steps toward them. "Welcome. Welcome." She herded them inside with all the expertise of a cowhand.

"There," Zach muttered for her ears only as they hurried

down the aisle toward an empty pew. "Was that welcome enough for you?"

"I never doubted Etta's welcome." She dipped her head as she slid in beside Zach, aware of shifting around them as people turned to stare. "Do I have a dirty face?" she whispered to Zach.

He turned to study her.

She clung to his dark gaze even as he grinned. "No dirt. Hair's in order. Clothes are proper. What more could you ask for?"

Then Reverend Williams took his place and her discomfort was soon forgotten as the familiarity of the hymns and the preacher's gentle words of wisdom touched her soul.

At her side, Zach locked his hands together in his lap. From outward appearances he seemed at ease, but she sensed an unfamiliar tightness in him. He must have sat here many times with Esther at his side. She lay her hand over his forearm and squeezed. Quickly, she pulled back, her cheeks burning. But her reward was in seeing him relax.

The service over, they rose to leave. Addie rushed to her side, dragging a friend with her.

"Irene, this is Minnie Stanwell. She's a good friend of mine." Addie took Irene's arm and drew her toward another clutch of women.

Irene shot a pleading look to Zach, but he only grinned like it was a huge joke.

Addie put her through a whirlwind of introductions. Irene's thoughts swam in a sea of strange names and faces and invitations to "come visit anytime."

She almost threw her arms around Zach's neck when he ambled over, two little boys beside him, and said, "We best be heading home."

She waited until they headed out of town to turn to him. "I think you enjoyed seeing me swallowed up by Addie's friends."

He chuckled. "There was quite a swarm of them, all right." He grew thoughtful. "But I doubt you were in much danger of being swallowed. Seems to me you're a young woman who can hold her own."

"Hmm." It sounded like a compliment. She settled back, easier in mind.

Over breakfast the next day, Zach announced, "I'll start plowing today." He turned from one boy to the other. "I'll be close enough you can see me, but I don't want you boys coming out. Matt is feeling his oats."

Irene knew Matt was the big-footed horse she had seen in the field.

Zach turned to her. "I hate to ask it, but could you bring me something cold to drink midmorning?"

"I'd love to." She noticed the flicker in his eyes and wondered if she'd been too enthusiastic. "Wouldn't we, boys?"

Two heads nodded vigorously.

"Good-bye then." He nodded at Irene and ruffled the boys' hair.

Harry and Donald stared after him like he had announced he would be gone until Christmas.

"No time to sit and mope." She scooped up dishes and plunged them into the dishwater. "If we're going to get cookies made in time to take them to your dad we're going to need to hurry."

"Oh boy! Can we help?" Harry asked for them both.

"I couldn't manage without you. Harry, you get the big mixing bowl. Donald, you bring me the baking sheets."

She let them help mix the dough, then showed them how to shape the cookies into balls, smiling as they labored over the task. Some cookies would be bigger, some smaller, but what difference did it make? They'd taste all the better for the love going into them.

By midmorning, the cookies lay golden and warm on a wire rack.

"Wash up now. It's time to go see Dad."

When they had done as she instructed, she handed Harry the sack of cookies and gave Donald a sack with four cups in it. She carried the jar of water.

The smell of freshly turned earth met them as they approached the field. Zach plowed down the side toward them. He waved, acknowledging them. Irene set the water on the grass and plunked down beside it as Zach continued his work.

The boys left their sacks with her so they could play in the cool furrows.

Zach had removed his shirt, giving her a chance to see his arm muscles ripple as he steadied the plow. She dipped her gaze, ashamed at the way she stared at him. But seconds later, she again watched him.

He drew close enough for her to see his eyes, and she knew he had seen her staring. Suddenly, it hit her. She had the right to stare. He was her husband. Even if in name only. She met his gaze steadily, refusing to turn away.

He turned away, hung the reins over the handle, grabbed up his shirt, and shrugged into it.

The boys waited until he stepped across the furrows before they launched themselves at him.

"Dad, Dad! We made cookies!" Harry shouted.

Donald, wrapped around Zach's leg, feet planted on one boot, rode high with his father's every step.

"Cookies? Great. I'm hungry." As Irene tried to get to her feet, he bent, caught her hand, and pulled her up, only inches away from him. His expression thoughtful, he smiled.

Determined to calm her wayward thoughts, she smiled. "Hope you like oatmeal cookies."

"I like any kind."

"Me, too." Harry handed her the sacks. She pulled out the cups and filled them with water, handing around the sack of cookies.

Zach stretched out on the grass. "Delicious," he murmured, having downed three in seconds. "Slow down, boys," he admonished as they each reached for a third.

Irene laughed. "Doesn't matter the age, the way to a man's heart is through his stomach."

Zach grinned. "Can't argue with that. Our stomachs thank you. Don't they, boys?" His warm words and equally warm smile played havoc with her determination to control the way her heart lurched when he looked at her like that.

The cookies had disappeared. The boys returned to digging in the dirt with sticks, but Zach seemed inclined to linger, twirling a blade of grass in his fingers.

Irene sat toying with her cup, so aware of his nearness that she was unable for the life of her to think of anything to say.

Finally, he pushed to his feet. "The plowing waits." He paused, waiting until she lifted her face to meet his gaze. "Thank you. I appreciate it. My stomach appreciates it. See you at dinner."

"Yes." Even after he turned away, she felt the intensity of his gaze. She waited until he resumed plowing before she called the boys.

That night they lay in bed, Zach on his back, hands behind his head, his elbow tickling her hair. She sensed something bothered him and waited for him to speak.

Finally, he sighed. "I worry about the boys."

She smiled into the gray light—not quite light, yet not dark enough to totally hide them from each other. She had only to shift her head slightly to see him stretched out beside her, his profile silhouetted against the window. His admission came as no great surprise. "I noticed."

"Suppose you did. But I mean forever and ever."

Startled by his words, she turned on her side so she could watch him. "What do you mean?"

"I wonder if they will ever be all right again." In the darkness, she could not tell his expression but felt his desperation.

"I remember once when I found a sparrow in the garden," she said. "I thought it was injured, but perhaps it was more frightened than anything. At any rate, it didn't have the strength to fly away, and I had no trouble catching the poor little thing."

He listened intently.

"I took it to the house, wrapped it in cotton, and fed it sugar water with a dropper. Father told me it was wrong to try to tame it. He said to put it outside. The best thing I could do, he said, was put it in a safe place and leave it be so it would get the nerve to fly again. I, of course, would not be persuaded."

He grunted. "Of course."

"Just as Father said, the bird died." She fell silent. After a moment, she sighed and added, "Maybe it would have lived if I'd done as Father suggested."

"Who knows? But what has that to do with my boys?"

"I was thinking of Donald. I think once he feels safe, he will fly again. Harry, well, Harry I'd like to see a little less serious, but perhaps like father, like son."

"I wasn't always so serious." Zach's quiet admission startled Irene.

"How were you, then?" She tried to imagine a less serious Zach and failed.

"I liked a good joke. Still do."

"Yes?"

"And I like to do fun things."

This new side of Zach intrigued her. "Such as?"

"Things." His voice turned cold.

She knew the conversation was over, but she wanted to ask what happened to that side of Zach. Only, of course, she knew the answer. Losing a wife had taken the fun from him.

"You're good for the boys," Zach mumbled.

"Zach, thank you for saying that." Her throat tightened. "You don't know how much it means to me." She reached for his arm, finding it under the covers. "I want so much to make a difference in their lives." Her voice dropping to a whisper, she added, "In your life."

He grunted and turned away. Within moments, his breathing deepened.

But Irene lay staring into the dusky shadows for a long time, hugging his words to her. Nothing else mattered but making these boys fly again. *Except,* a stubborn voice inside her argued, *making Zach laugh.* She refused to allow her thoughts to wander any further and closed her eyes, willing sleep to come.

☙

Zach plowed for several days, then started seeding, the discer cutting neat finger tracks through the sod. He worked long hours, leaving as soon as it was light, returning in time for a late supper. Irene began to rise early in order to make his breakfast before he left. The time alone with him held a magical quality as they watched morning dawn.

"It will be a hot one," Zach announced as the sky shifted from gray to hard blue. "I hope the weather holds until I get the crop in the ground."

"How much longer?"

"Three more days if the weather holds and the discer doesn't break."

"I never realized before how hard a farmer works." Zach spent long hours in the field no matter how hot or windy. He fell into bed so weary he barely sighed before he fell asleep.

"Got to take advantage of the good weather. Look, there they go."

Every morning two deer with spotted fawns tiptoeing after them made their way across the valley floor, disappearing like the morning mists into the trees. She leaned forward to get a better view. "I can't imagine life being much better than this."

He sat back, studying her narrowly. "This is nothing to write home about."

Stung by his hard tone, she sat back in her chair. "How can you say that? We have the best view in the world. You said so yourself. The air is sweet and pure. We live in blissful peace. The boys are well and healthy. The farm is productive. Seems to me everything is buttons and bows. What more could you want?"

His dark gaze bored into her. She felt the hunger of her heart answering his demanding look and bit her lower lip. She leaned toward him. His eyes darkened with purpose. He slid his elbows forward. Then as suddenly as slamming a door, his eyes shuttered, and he pushed back from the table. "There's more," he muttered, jerking to his feet. He slapped his hat on his head and left.

Irene dropped her head to her hands. How could she have been so naive to think she could marry a man, eat with him, talk with him, sleep beside him, and not end up wanting more from him? Did she think she could lock her emotions in a box?

She didn't know what she'd thought, but having given her word to enter into a marriage of convenience only, she had no right to ache for more. But all her arguing did not change the way she felt. Despite her promise, despite her resolve, she had grown to love this man. She understood her love would never be returned, would never find satisfaction in the tenderness she ached for.

"Please, God, help me turn my love into acts of service. Help me contain my emotions."

ↄ

A chill wind drove Irene and the boys indoors early. Zach had told her at dinner he would not return until he finished. He wanted to finish before the weather turned.

"It's time for bed," she told the boys as they hurried in out of the cold.

The boys ground to a halt and stared at her.

"Where's Dad?" Harry demanded.

"You heard him say he wouldn't be in until he finished," she explained patiently.

"Do we have to go to bed before he comes in?"

"Yes, you do."

Donald stuck his fingers in his mouth and watched his brother.

Harry sighed. "I suppose it's all right."

Irene grabbed them in a hug and tickled them. "I suppose it is."

Donald squirmed out of her reach. She tickled Harry harder as he giggled. She knew he liked it. Often when she stopped, he sidled up to her begging for more. After a minute, she straightened. "If you hurry and get your pajamas on, I'll read you a new story."

Harry needed no second invitation and scampered for his room. Irene and Donald followed more slowly. As soon as they were ready, she went to her trunk and found the book she wanted.

"Harry, you climb into bed." She waited while he obeyed, then lay beside him, pulling Donald into the crook of her arm, covering him with a quilt. She paused to stuff some pillows under her head, then she opened the book.

"Tom Sawyer by Mark Twain."

She read a whole chapter, but when she quit, Harry begged for more. Donald had fallen asleep, and she pulled her arm out from under him, shifting about until she found a comfortable position between the boys.

She read until she was sure Harry had fallen asleep.

She startled when Zach shook her shoulder. She smiled up at him. "You're back."

"Shh," he warned, pointing at the sleeping boys on either side of her. He slid his arms under Donald and lifted him to his own cot.

She slipped from the bed and stood beside Zach looking down at the children. "So sweet," she whispered.

He took her by the hand and led her from the room, across the hall to their bedroom where he turned to face her, his expression soft. "Were the boys upset because I wasn't here to put them to bed?"

She shook her head. "They asked after you but didn't fuss."

His eyes grew hard. "Donald never sleeps anywhere but his own cot."

Unsettled by his shift in mood, she attempted to explain. "He fell asleep while I was reading."

"Get ready for bed." He strode from the room.

She hurriedly pulled her clothes off and slipped into her nightgown, then climbed into bed. Knowing Zach would not come to bed until the room was dark, she turned off the lantern without reading her Bible.

He strode in, undressed in the dark, and slipped under the covers, his back to her as he clung to his side of the bed.

"Why are you angry with me?" she asked after a few minutes of stiff silence.

"I'm not."

"I'm sorry. I didn't know you opposed Donald sleeping in Harry's bed." It seemed unusual, but it was his house and his children, which entitled him to make whatever rules he wished.

"I'm not against it." He spoke slowly like she was a half-witted child. "But he has not fallen asleep anywhere but his own bed since. . ." He broke off. When he resumed, his voice was hard as iron. "Since their mother."

"Oh, I see," she whispered. And indeed she did. Again she had inadvertently upset the pattern laid down by his first wife. "I told you before I can't take her place. I can only be me." She despised the pleading in her voice. She didn't want to plead. She wanted him to accept her as she was because. . . She closed her eyes and tried to ignore the truth. She wanted him to accept her because he cared about her. "I'm sorry," she added, though she couldn't say if she was sorry for him with his lost dreams, or herself with her hopeless longings. Or the boys who were stuck with two adults who couldn't even sort their own lives out, let alone help two children do so.

"Leave it be," he mumbled, already half asleep.

She nodded in the darkness. This was not the time to be trying to sort out the complexity of her role. As sleep claimed her, she wondered if there was any way to sort things out so everyone was satisfied.

The next morning, black clouds scudded across the sky, driven before a wind that seemed to come directly from the snow-laden mountains.

"I'll work the garden this morning," Zach announced over breakfast. He had given her a measuring look when he first got up, then he settled into his easy, familiar behavior. "If it don't rain, we might get it planted today."

"I found a tin of seeds in the pantry, and I've brought some with me." She was willing to let bygones be bygones. Life was too short to harbor ill will.

A little later, she heard him behind the house and hurried to the bedroom to watch out the window. Donald and Harry crowded around her. "Now we'll be able to eat like kings, won't we?" Harry asked.

She chuckled. "In a little while. It takes time for plants to grow." She ruffled his hair. "Just like it does boys."

He stretched to his full height. "See how tall I'm getting."

She studied him critically. "I believe you've grown an inch since I got here. Those pants are way too short for you. We're going to have to see about finding you more clothes."

Donald pressed into her leg, and she smiled down at him. "Why, look how big you're getting. And your pants are too small, too." She clucked her tongue and shook her head. "You two better slow down, or you'll be right out of your clothes."

Donald's eyes sparkled.

Her gaze returned to Zach, her heart swelling with a now-familiar longing.

She pressed her forehead to the cool glass, unable to tear herself away from studying the man she loved. How many days would she watch him unobserved, loving the way he moved? She bit her bottom lip as she silently answered her question with another. How many days are there in a lifetime? A lifetime of longing and wanting. She straightened. Even though her love would never be returned, there was too much good in life to waste it pining for what could never be.

Zach finished and turned the horse toward the barn.

The house was suddenly small and hot. "Put on your coats," she told the boys. "We'll go have a look."

At the garden, she scooped up a handful of earth and smelled it. So rich and moist. So full of promise. *If only my relationship with Zach could be that way*, she mused. *Instead of written on a heart of stone.*

"It worked up good."

Zach's voice behind her made her start. Her cheeks warmed to be caught thinking about him, but she reminded herself, he couldn't read her thoughts. She forced a deep breath into her trembling insides. "It's a fine garden spot."

He stood beside her. "I'm sorry about last night." His words were low so the boys wouldn't hear.

She stared straight ahead, not knowing quite what he meant.

"I don't expect you to be Esther. I don't even want you to be."

His admission so surprised her that she spun around and stared at him. The look on his face made her wonder if his admission had shocked him as much as her.

"What do you want?" She hadn't meant to sound so urgent.

He rubbed his hand across the back of his neck and shrugged. "I told you. A housekeeper and someone to care for the boys." But he sounded more confused than convinced.

She held his gaze, searching it for clues about his feelings and saw only a reflection of her own uncertainty and hesitation.

"If you don't mind working in the cold—"

"I'll get the seeds." She rushed to the house.

A bit later, Irene bent over her row of carrots, sprinkling the seed carefully on the rich soil, raking a covering over. Donald followed her like a shadow.

On the other side of the garden, Zach and Harry planted potatoes.

Working had a leveling affect on her emotions, and she wondered why she worried herself with a desire for more when she already had so much; a lovely home with the best view in the world, two darling little boys, and a big, strong husband. Life was so good.

She began to sing, "I'm always chasing rainbows." Quietly at first, then as her well-being returned, louder, not caring what Zach would think. When his deep voice joined in, she faltered and spun around to face him.

He leaned on his shovel, grinning as he sang, his eyes dark and teasing.

She remembered his words: *I wasn't always so serious.* She faced him across the plowed garden, drinking in the expression in his eyes. She smiled so widely she could hardly sing, and by the time they'd finished the verse, they were both laughing.

Still grinning, he dug the shovel into the soil and waited for Harry to drop in a piece of potato.

Irene turned back to her carrots, feeling lighter in heart than she had in a long time.

By the time they were done, the sun had broken through.

Irene stood beside Zach, looking with satisfaction at the stakes at the end of each row. "We'll soon be eating like kings," she said.

When Zach didn't answer, she turned to look at him, wondering what he was thinking. He stared at the garden, his expression troubled.

She followed his gaze, wondering if she'd forgotten something. But she could see nothing to give him concern. "What's wrong?"

Slowly, he brought his gaze to hers, and his expression smoothed. "Nothing," he muttered.

But she wasn't convinced. She'd caught a glimpse of something dark and distant in his eyes and guessed he was remembering. Her throat grew tight. It was like fighting a ghost.

At the rattle of an approaching wagon, they both turned toward the house.

"Sounds like company," he muttered.

"Who could it be?" She looked at her soiled hands and wrinkled her nose. "Is there dirt on my face?"

Zach turned and looked her over. "Here, I'll get it." He brushed her cheek.

She pressed her lips together and prayed her eyes wouldn't give her away.

A slow grin spread across his face. "I've made it worse."

"Fix it," she urged.

He bent his arm and rubbed at her cheek with his sleeve. His eyes were dark and gleaming. A pulse thudded along his cheekbone.

He lowered his arm, trailing his hand along her cheek, leaving his fingertips resting on her jaw.

She couldn't move. His touch sent long fingers into her heart and unlocked longings she was trying so hard to suppress.

"Irene, I—"

"Hello, there! The boys said you were out here." An unfamiliar voice shattered the moment.

Muffling a grunt, Zach spun to face the visitor. "Hello, Fred. How nice of you to visit."

Irene gathered her exploding senses together and stepped to Zach's side as he introduced Fred and Dorothy Spinks. "Neighbors to the east," he explained.

She nodded to the couple, studiously avoiding Zach's eyes. "Do come in for tea."

seven

"How are you getting on?" Dorothy Spinks perched on the edge of her chair, holding the teacup daintily.

"Fine, thank you." Irene wondered if someone had told Dorothy extending the little finger as she drank proved her a refined person. She stuck it out with the doggedness of a stubborn argument.

"The boys must be quite a handful."

Irene smiled. "Harry and Donald? No. They're both dears."

Dorothy gave her a narrow-eyed look. "I heard tell Donald doesn't talk."

Irene's smile never faltered though her patience was growing thinner by the minute. "He's a man of few words." She wished Zach would come back, but Fred had asked to borrow a piece of leather to fix something or other.

Dorothy, not to be discouraged, plowed onward. "It's a shame. It really is."

Irene sipped her tea, determined not to take the bait.

"We all said so at the time." Dorothy cast her a hopeful look, no doubt wanting to see a spark of interest in Irene's eyes.

Irene's smile felt starched. She knew Dorothy would continue whether or not she said a word. "Is that a fact?"

Dorothy nodded vigorously enough to rattle her cup and saucer. "A crying shame. I never did understand why Zach felt he had to join the war." She sniffed. "In the end, they fought and won without his help."

Irene pinched the handle of the cup so hard she feared it would snap. How dare this person sit as Zach's judge and jury!

The woman across from her sniffed loudly. "She was never strong. He should have seen it. The rest of us did." She was gathering up a head of steam. "But you know what men are like. They can't see what's right in front of them unless it jumps up and grabs them by the nose. And poor Esther wasn't one to push herself forward. She was a sweet, gentle girl. Not strong, mind you. He should have never left her on her own. It was asking too much."

Unable to take any more, Irene jumped to her feet. "More tea?" She shoved the plate of cookies toward the woman. "Have another cookie."

"Don't mind if I do."

She caught the sound of men's voices and rushed to the door, practically ready to throw herself into Zach's arms, she was so grateful to see him.

He gave her a strange look then grinned. She knew he had read her desperation. "Fred brought the mail." He handed her a bundle of letters and papers.

"Thank you so much."

She looked behind the men. "Where are the boys?"

"I said they could stay and play with the kittens."

She nodded and closed the door, turning to Fred. "Would you care for more tea?"

Fred shook his head. "No thanks. We need to be getting back home. Come along, Dorothy."

The woman swallowed the last of her tea and rose. "I'm so glad for this chance to visit." She took Irene's hand. "Remember, we're close by if you ever need anything." She squeezed Irene's hand.

Irene waited until the door closed behind them before she dropped into the closest chair.

Zach chuckled. "Did she manage to squeeze your life story from you? Esther said the woman was like a bee buzzing around for something juicy to light on."

Irene shook her head. "I think this was a fishing trip."

He raised his eyebrows.

"She was fishing for information. Not that she got any. Mostly I said, 'Is that so?' and she'd be off again."

"I 'spect she's harmless enough. Fred's a good man." He

reached for another cookie and took the bundle of mail.

Irene didn't bother saying she thought Dorothy was anything but harmless going around making accusations and sowing seeds of doubt.

"Some letters for you."

She took them.

The boys clattered in, pressing around her. "You got letters?" Harry asked.

"Yes, one from Grace and one from my father."

Two pairs of eyes looked up at her.

"Would you like to know what they say?"

Two heads nodded.

"Boys, that's Irene's private business," Zach warned.

"I don't mind. If there's anything I don't want to share I'll simply skip reading it." She tore open Grace's letter first and skimmed it. "She says she and Billy are doing well. She went to the theater and says it is lovely. She says Billy was talking to Wop May."

"Who's Wop May?" Harry demanded.

"A Canadian pilot who shot down some of the German airplanes." She thought of the many stories Billy had brought them.

"Wow." Harry was duly impressed.

"He was in the final fight with the Red Baron, one of Germany's best pilots."

Zach grinned at his son. "Sounds like fun, doesn't it?"

"I heard that the Canadians were some of the best pilots."

"Why would that be, I wonder?" Zach asked.

"More nerve than brains, maybe."

He chuckled at her dry assessment. "Oh, we Canadians are a notorious lot."

Harry raced around the room, his arms out, dipping and soaring like an airplane.

Irene glanced through the rest of the letter and folded it away.

Zach sorted through the other items; she opened her

father's letter, smiling as she read how he was seeing one of the nurses she had worked with.

"Good news?" Zach asked.

She nodded and told him. "No wonder he couldn't wait to get two grown daughters off his hands."

"You don't mind?"

"Surprisingly enough, I don't. He deserves whatever happiness he can find."

⊱

"It's time to think about fixing some clothes for you boys."

"I got new pants before Dad went to war," Harry said. "He bought them just before we said good-bye to him at the train station."

She stared at Harry. It was the first time he'd spoken of his past. Hoping he'd say more, she asked, "What pants were those?"

"I'll show you." He led her to the bedroom and dug into his bottom drawer, pulling out a wrinkled pair of brown trousers and handing them to her.

She shook them. They looked as good as new. "Why, they've hardly been worn."

He nodded, his eyes never leaving her face. "I never wore them."

"Why ever not?"

His bottom lip quivered, and she knelt in front of him, taking his hands. "Was there some reason you didn't wear them?"

He nodded.

"Can you tell me?"

Again he nodded, but he didn't speak. Donald sidled up to him and pressed into his side. Harry took a shaky breath. "Mommy said we would never see Dad again."

"Ah, I see." She saw many things—the fear that made him cling to a pair of trousers as insurance against his father's return, the uncertainty of a young mother who feared she would never see her husband again. A haunting ache filled her. She had not seen her husband again, but it was she who'd left, not Zach.

"But your daddy came back. Why have you never worn them?"

"I couldn't."

She waited, but he said no more, and she stood up, wondering what strange thoughts filled this child's head. "Can you wear them now?"

"I think they're too small."

Holding them against him to measure, she had to agree. "I guess I'll have to adjust them for Donald."

Harry relaxed, knowing he would never have to wear them. Somehow, although she didn't understand it, he seemed to associate Zach's leaving and his mother's death with this piece of clothing.

"What else do we have? May I look through your drawers and see?"

Harry nodded.

She sorted his clothing into separate piles; mending, things too small but fixable for Donald, and those for Donald to grow into. Then she sorted through Donald's clothing. The mending pile grew rapidly. "Now where will we find yard goods so I can make you each new trousers and shirts? Something nice to wear to town."

"In the big chest?" Harry suggested. "The one in the hall."

"Of course." She lifted the lid, surprised at the size of it. "It's as big as a small house."

Harry laughed. "For real small people."

She grinned at him. "Now don't you be saucy." She ruffled his hair to show she wasn't angry.

A woman's heavy winter coat lay on top, and she held it up. Talk about small people! This would be small even for Grace. "Was this your mama's?"

Harry nodded.

She studied it for possibilities, then set it aside, exploring further. A stack of photos. She turned the top one over. A family picture with Zach, a woman, and a babe in arms. She bent to examine it. Esther had been a tiny woman. She glanced at Harry. "You look like her." He leaned over her shoulder and looked at the picture.

"That's me as a baby," he said.

"I thought so. I wish I could see you better. I'd like to see you as a baby."

He picked up the other pictures and chose one, handing it to her. "Here."

"Oh. You're so adorable." Dressed in white rompers, posed on a wicker chair, his brown eyes looked back at her, the same solemn expression she'd grown familiar with. "You still have the same look in your eyes."

He watched her. "Was I really adorable?"

She lowered the picture and met his gaze. "Yes, you were. And you know something?"

"What?"

"You still are." She hugged him.

He leaned into her with a desperation that made her heart ache.

"Didn't you know that?" She stroked his hair, overcome with love for this child.

He shook his head.

"Then listen while I tell you again." She held him so she could look into his face. "Harry Marshall, you are a lovely child. I think you are wonderful. I'm so glad I came to be your mother."

Harry nodded, then turned back to the pictures. "Here's one of Donald." He handed it to her. "What do you think of it?"

She ran her finger over the likeness, her smile widening. Donald, grinning at the camera, seemed about to explode into mischief. He had gone to the bedroom; she called him. "Donald, come and see yourself."

He stood in the doorway, eyes wary.

"It's a picture of you as a baby. Look."

He sidled up to her and leaned his dark head over the picture. Three fingers slid into his mouth.

"You are so sweet. I don't think I have ever seen a nicer smile." She chucked him under the chin. "Where are you hiding that smile, young man?"

He patted his tummy.

She grabbed him and tickled his stomach. "I guess I'll have to tickle it out of you, then."

He smiled, but it was a cautious shadow of the one in the picture.

She let him go. "What else do we have in here?"

Harry handed her another picture. "This is when Mom and Dad got married."

Esther smiled sweetly at the camera. Zach gazed adoringly at his new wife; his smile spoke volumes of pride and joy.

Irene touched his face wondering if his smile was hidden in his stomach, too.

The kitchen door slammed.

Irene glanced up. Was it dinnertime already? Zach strode into the narrow hall.

"What are you doing?" His voice was hard.

"I was looking for yard goods to make the boys new clothes. We found these pictures and were looking at them."

"Put them away."

She nodded, struck dumb by his harshness. The boys shrank back against her. Quickly, she gathered the pictures together, set them back in the chest, and closed it. This needed discussing, but not while the boys were present.

She hurried to the kitchen and served up the soup and bread she'd prepared earlier. She glanced around the table, determined not to let the heavy atmosphere prevail. "Has anyone seen our deer lately?"

All eyes turned toward the window.

"I saw them this morning, sliding into the trees," Zach said.

"I haven't seen them in days. How big are the fawns now?"

"They're still little shadows following the doe. By the way, that reminds me. You boys better check on your kittens today. I think they're getting big enough to climb out of the manger."

Harry and Donald looked at each other, exchanging some

silent message. Harry turned to his dad. "Can we bring them to the house?"

Zach gave his sons a sober look. "You can bring them for a visit but only for a few minutes. They need to be with their mother yet, and I don't want them hanging around underfoot."

Harry grinned at Donald.

Irene waited until dinner was over and the boys had raced off toward the barn before she confronted Zach. "I don't mean to be putting my nose where it doesn't belong. My only intention was to do the mending and fix some clothes for the boys. I'm sure you've noticed that their clothes are in need of repair. And both boys have their ankles and wrists sticking out by inches. But if there are things you don't want me touching, say so."

He sighed. "Touch anything you like. Just don't bring those pictures out. That's a part of my life that is over and done with. The past is past."

He was wrong. That part of his life controlled him and his sons to such an extent they no longer knew how to smile and enjoy life. "Is that why your smile has disappeared? And Donald's? And why Harry is fearful? Because the past is past?"

He pushed his chair back, the sound sending pinpricks down her spine. "I don't want you touching that part of my life."

She stifled a cry, stung by his rejection. How could she ever hope to become part of his life if he shut her out of such a large portion? She straightened her shoulders. "If that's your wish, so be it." She meant to remain calm and cool, but the thought of all that pain left untended was too much for her. "But you're making a mistake. Both you and the boys need to talk about your loss and deal with it."

His hard look made her shiver. "Thank you for your learned advice, but we have our own way of dealing with it." He jerked to his feet and strode from the house.

Irene watched him cross the yard in long, angry strides. She stared long after he'd disappeared from sight. She should have kept silent. Their relationship did not allow a free exchange of opinions. But her feelings for Zach and the boys precluded keeping silent. She saw how they were all hurting, and she wanted nothing more than to help.

"Please, God. Help me to keep quiet when I should. Grant me wisdom to speak when it's the right time—and patience with this situation."

She cleaned up from the meal, then collected the mending and pulled out the sewing machine she'd found in the cupboard behind the door in the bedroom. She'd learned to use such a machine during the war and thanked Esther for having one.

She had repaired several shirts when the boys returned with their arms full of kittens. She left her task to admire and play with the kittens.

"I better take them back now," Harry said. "Come on, Donald, you can help."

Irene returned to the pile of mending, and the boys returned to play outside where they could spend hours constructing an intricate, tiny farm from twigs and stones and a bag of marbles.

The afternoon settled around them, warm and lazy.

Suddenly, Donald stood at her elbow.

"I never heard you come in."

He handed her a shapeless object.

"What do you have?" She examined it. It was soiled and torn, but it was obviously a stuffed bear. She looked at him, trying to understand what he wanted. "You want me to fix it?"

He nodded.

"I'll do my best. Is it something special?"

To her utter shock, his eyes filled with tears. She scooped him into her arms and hugged him, rocking back and forth as she murmured. "Poor little man." Her heart was irretrievably linked to this child. He might not have been created under her heart, but he had been born in her heart. She loved him so fiercely she could not stop the tears from trickling down her cheeks, dripping into the dark hair of this precious child.

He let her hold him a moment longer, then pushed away, giving the ragged toy a pat before he rejoined his brother.

She labored over the toy, painstakingly fixing the many

tears. One place required a patch as the material had rotted. After she had the shape restored, she scrubbed it carefully. Finally satisfied, she used two clothespins to hang it on the wire line behind the stove where she normally hung the dish towels to dry.

Donald slipped inside as she finished.

"I've just hung it to dry." She pointed to the toy.

He walked over and touched it before he gave a tiny grateful smile and went back outside.

When Zach came in for supper, a boy clasped in each hand, Donald hurried over to the stuffed toy.

"It's not dry yet, but you can have it if you like." When he nodded, Irene unclipped it.

Donald took it and climbed up into his chair while Irene set the serving dishes on the table. "I've made your favorites. . ." She broke off at the startled look on Harry's face. "What's wrong?"

"Where did that come from?" The child pointed at Donald's toy.

Irene shrugged. "Donald brought it to me and wanted me to fix it." Harry's expression puzzled her. "Is something wrong?" She looked at Zach who watched Donald with puzzlement. "What is it?" she demanded.

Zach shrugged. "It was his favorite toy. He carried it everywhere with him. He had it under his arm when I left to join the army, but I never saw it again. Until now. I wondered what happened to it."

Irene turned to Donald. He clutched the worn toy, his fingers entrenched in his mouth. "There's only one person who knows where it was, and he's not telling."

"I don't suppose it matters after all. Pass the potatoes, please." Zach turned his attention to the meal.

But Irene saw the way Harry stared at Donald, and she wondered.

≈

"It's a cold wind tonight." Zach leaned over to shut the window above the table. "Looks like we're finally going to get that rain."

Irene stared out the window at the lowering clouds obliterating the mountains. "If it means the weather will clear, I'll be grateful. I miss the clear blue sky and the sight of my mountains." She ignored his raised eyebrows. "What's the point in having the best view in the world if one can't see it?"

He lit the lantern and pulled his chair close to read the papers while she darned one of his socks.

Finally, she stretched and yawned. "I'll be off to bed now."

He glanced up briefly. "Good night."

The chill wind coming through the narrow opening of the window made Irene shiver into her nightgown and pull the covers up to her chin. She propped her Bible on her knee so she could huddle under the covers as she read. As she began to pray, her wishes sprang to the forefront of her thoughts. How she longed to see the little boys laugh as they should; how she yearned for more of a relationship with Zach. Plain and simple, she wanted his love. "Lord, if it be possible," she whispered.

Slipping one arm out, she turned the lantern off and huddled back under the covers. A few minutes later, Zach entered. The first thing he did was close the window. "You trying to freeze us?" he muttered as he dashed into bed.

Over the weeks, they had settled into an ease with each other that allowed her to shuffle about without worrying if she bumped into him. She knew he was awake as he lay on his back, his arms above the covers. She waited, knowing he would speak when he was ready, but also understanding that he didn't always wish to share his thoughts.

"Did you think Harry seemed—I don't know—almost worried about Donald's stuffed bear?"

"I thought it a little odd."

"I wonder where it was." He shuffled under the covers. "I guess it doesn't matter."

Thunder crashed. Irene jerked to a sitting position. Before she could calm her racing heart, a flash of lightning filled the room with blue light. Another deafening roll of thunder followed closely.

"Dad! Dad!" Harry raced into the room, pulling Donald by the hand. In the next flash of liquid fire, the boys' eyes stood out like black coal.

Zach lifted the covers, letting in a draft of cold air. "Wondered how long you'd be."

The boys jumped in, burrowing under the covers as thunder rolled down the mountains like a landslide of gigantic rocks. The sound died away, rebounding in Irene's heart.

The heavenly fireworks continued for a long time. Rain slanted across the window in icy splatters.

Harry squealed with each ensuing clap of thunder, clinging to Zach. Donald burrowed against Irene, sucking his fingers with a thin slurping sound that surged in the moments of quiet to be silenced by the horrendous noise.

Conversation was impossible. Irene hugged Donald, cradling his head, pressing her hands to his head in a futile attempt to block out the noise. His body stiffened with each thunderous clap.

Then the lightning faded into the distance; the thunder rolled more softly.

"It's passed over." Zach's deep voice assured them all was well. Irene's arms ached from holding the child in her arms. She relaxed.

"Can we sleep here?" Harry's muffled voice asked.

"For awhile."

Irene shifted to make more room, reaching to touch Harry and assure him of her presence.

Zach moaned. "It's a tight fit for us all." He shuffled about and threw his arm around Harry, trapping Irene's arm beneath the weight of his own.

Her insides shivered, but not from cold. The fluttering of her nerves trickled along Zach's arm. His muscle twitched, but he did not pull away. Rather, he patted her shoulder and whispered, "Everybody go to sleep."

eight

The day was the fairest she'd seen since her arrival in Alberta; a breeze teased her with alluring scents of grass and sage, roses, and the soap scent that clung to Zach. She blocked the direction of her thoughts and forced them back to nature. The sky was as blue and clear as a fine china plate; the sun, neither too hot, nor too weak, touched her skin like a caress. Her mind shifted back to Zach.

Stop it, Irene ordered herself. *Stop tormenting yourself with aimless longings. Enjoy the day.*

"Is it really the biggest event of the year?" she asked, clutching at conversation in order to corral her thoughts.

"For the summer, at least. I suppose the Christmas concert is equally important."

"What are the expectations from me at this community picnic? What will I do?"

Harry leaned between them; Donald curled up in her lap.

"What do you want to do?" Zach's voice teased in a way that made her keep her eyes on the right ear of the horse in front of her.

"There's races," Harry offered. He had bounced with excitement for almost a week since Addie had cornered Zach in the churchyard and bothered him until he gave his promise he would take the family to the community picnic.

"They didn't go last year," she'd pointed out. "They can't miss two years in a row."

"I couldn't take them last year. I wasn't here." He'd crossed his arms over his chest and stared down at his sister.

"That was last year." Addie had pressed her face closer to Zach's. "This is this year."

"Gets harder to fool you every year," he'd drawled.

106

"Don't try to get me off in a different direction. I'm not letting you go until you give your word."

Irene grinned at the idea of Addie stopping Zach from doing anything he set his mind to. Her smile deepened, sending warm trails down her insides when Zach had met her look and winked, acknowledging the futility of Addie's threat.

"Guess I better give my word then, or we'll stand here until we starve." His gaze had lingered on Irene as he spoke to his sister. She'd felt caught in a warm, liquid state.

"You promise?" Addie had insisted.

He'd dropped his gaze to his sister. Irene's legs had gone limp, but she'd forced herself to stand straight and calm.

Addie had spun around to Irene. "It's a picnic. We all bring sandwiches, cake, pickles—stuff like that—and share it." She'd rattled on about the importance of the event. "Everyone goes. It's a great time. I know you'll like it."

It wasn't until they rode toward home that Irene had begun to collect her thoughts. "It sounds wonderful," she'd said.

"Addie obviously thinks it's as important as the right to vote." His dry tone had not disguised the pleasure he had in Addie.

"I hope I got all the instructions." She'd repeated them to Zach.

"Sounds about right to me."

Harry, upon hearing they were to attend the picnic, filled in more information for Irene. "We have all sorts of races. Even for big people like you."

She'd laughed at the concession.

Small wonder she began to think of the community picnic as something akin to a coronation.

"I still don't know if I'm dressed correctly." Thinking of the lawn parties back home, she chose a fine white dress and put the boys in dark trousers and nice white shirts.

Zach ran his gaze over her length, finally meeting her eyes, a gleam making his sparkle. "I think you look very nice." He grinned. "And appropriate."

Her mouth refused to function as his gaze drew her into a land of flowers, perfume, and warmth. It wasn't until he turned his attention back to the horse that she could gather her thoughts back to the reality of Donald's weight against her arm, the hard bench pressing into her legs, and the sharp odor of the horse.

"I never paid much attention to what women wear," Zach said in a slow way, "but seems to me they dress much like you for this event." He emphasized the last word in such a way she understood him to mean it was only a picnic.

"It's not the crowning of a king?" She sounded slightly shocked.

He laughed. "Hey. Far as I know, we've never even had the Prime Minister attend. So relax and enjoy yourself."

"You're right. I intend to have a great deal of fun." She smiled to herself. Why wouldn't she? A long lazy afternoon with Zach at her side; the boys playing with their friends—it sounded idyllic.

Long before they reached the grassy field, she saw the rows of buggies and horses and a few automobiles. As they drew closer, she saw groups of people scattered about the area and caught a glimpse through the trees of several others walking along the river. Upon close observation, she saw many of the women dressed as she, with the older women in darker, heavier colors.

Zach pulled the wagon into the row. He took Donald from her and set him on the ground, then reached up to help her. His hands lingered at her waist as they looked into each other's eyes. "See. It's just a bunch of people down by the river. Everyone's come to enjoy the nice weather."

"Then why do you look so nervous?"

"I don't." He shook his head. "You see too much."

"Don't worry," she soothed. "I won't tell anyone." He took the food she'd prepared and slipped her hand through his arm as they marched across the grass toward the others. "It's only a group of people enjoying the weather," she reminded him, squeezing his arm to say she understood. There must be many places and times when he was suddenly confronted with memories of Esther. She held her head high, determined she would do everything in her power to make this a picnic for him to remember with fondness—not to blot out Esther's memory, but to give him fresh ones.

He set her two boxes on a large table where others had stacked their boxes of food, then headed her toward the river. "It's a beautiful spot for a walk."

She knew a walk through a set of corrals would seem beautiful if she could walk arm in arm with Zach like this. Donald and Harry traipsed after them, but she didn't mind. They were as entitled to this time of closeness as she.

They paused at the river's edge, watching the water meander on its way. Harry threw rocks while Donald stood quietly watching.

Then they turned to follow the path along the edge.

"It's so peaceful," she murmured. Voices of other like-minded people drifted to them, hushed by the river's gentle voice.

The channel turned a little, as did the path. Irene caught her toe on an exposed root and stumbled.

Zach caught her, his hands warm and firm on her arms.

Her breath tightened inside her as she stared into his dark eyes reflecting mysterious light off the river.

His hands tightened possessively. "Are you okay?" His voice seemed thick. Or was it only that her ears were clouded by the rumble of the river? The thunder of her heart? She nodded, too trapped by the light in his eyes to speak.

He pulled her closer, his gaze searching her face. "Irene," he murmured.

"Time for races!" a voice boomed from behind the trees. "Everybody up to the field for races." The voice faded as the intruder called up and down the length of the river.

"Come on, Dad. Hurry up." Harry jerked Zach's arm.

For a moment, Zach didn't move, his eyes clouding. Irene stepped back, brushing a strand of hair from her face. Did he regret the intrusion as much as she?

Harry raced back along the path, Donald trudging after

him. Zach and Irene followed more slowly. She hoped he would say something about what had just happened—almost happened. Or had she only imagined the look in his eyes?

People bunched together all over the field as they returned.

"Zach, you old rascal. We need someone to mark off the races. Come on and hold this rope." A man waved his arm at Zach, extending a length of rope.

"I'll be right there." Zach looked around. "There's Addie." He pointed to a group of young women. "Go stay with her."

Irene nodded though the bottom seemed to have fallen from her heart. She hadn't thought about having to be apart from Zach. "Come on, boys. Let's go find Aunt Addie."

Addie saw her coming and called, "You made it. I thought Zach might change his mind."

"Why would he do that?"

Addie shrugged. "Because he likes to be difficult. Always has." She smiled. "Maybe you'll be able to whip him into shape."

Irene laughed at the thought. "And what shape would you like him?"

"Maybe it isn't the shape I'd like to change as much as the stubborn attitude."

Irene gave Addie a sidelong look. "You don't fool me in the least. You wouldn't change a thing about him." *Nor would I. Except to have him love me.*

Addie had the grace to chuckle. "You're quite right. I'm very proud of my big brother." She drew Irene to her circle of friends, most of whom Irene had met at church.

Minnie welcomed her. "Are you enjoying the picnic?"

"Very much." Which wasn't quite the truth. What she had been enjoying was walking along the river with Zach. She watched him holding one end of the rope. His gaze found her among the other young women. A slow smile crossed his face, and he lifted one hand in silent greeting.

Although she felt like smiling from ear to ear, Irene gave a slight smile and nodded. It wouldn't do to draw attention to herself—or expose her unrequited love to others.

Addie grabbed her hand. "Come on." She crowded toward the center of the field. "The races are about to begin."

"Girls four and under," called a man who seemed to be in charge, and mothers dragged wee children to the rope.

Zach and his helper moved their rope to a few feet from the start line and lay it on the ground.

At the signal, amidst a roar of cheering, the little girls toddled toward a parent or friend, though some of the smaller ones fled to protective arms, the sudden noise and all those strangers too much for them.

As the noise subsided, Irene leaned over to speak to the little boy clutching her leg. "Do you want to go in a race, Donald?" She kept her voice low so the others wouldn't hear.

He shook his head, pressing more tightly to her.

"Then you don't have to. You can stay with me."

When the race for the little boys was announced, Addie turned toward Donald, but Irene caught her eye and shook her head. Addie nodded.

Knowing Zach would be concerned about his son, she sought him across the distance and shook her head ever so slightly. He nodded, his dark gaze grateful, then turned his attention back to the race.

Harry waited at the beginning line when the race for the nine- and ten-year-old boys was announced. Irene smiled at him and waved. Anyone looking at him would see nothing but a thin lad, too serious for such a fun occasion, but she saw the barely contained excitement in the way his hands clenched at his side and the quick wave he gave her before he turned his attention on the man who gave the signal to run.

Irene bent to Donald's side. "Harry's going to race to the rope your daddy's holding. Let's cheer him on." She yelled Harry's name as he raced across the field.

Harry didn't win. He was in the middle. He paused for a word with his father before coming to her, his eyes gleaming.

"You did great." She squeezed his shoulder.

There were races for every age, including one for married women.

"That's us." Addie grabbed her arm.

"I can't." Donald still clung to her leg, but Zach came over and took his son.

"You win for old England," he murmured.

"Well, put that way, I don't have much choice." She let Addie pull her to the start line, surprised at how many women, some not so young, were prepared to race against each other.

Then they were off. Irene ran as hard as she could, maintaining the lead by a slim margin. She'd almost reached the rope marking the finish line when the boys holding it took a step backward, then another, teasing the women.

"Martin, you stop that," one puffing woman called. "Or when I get home, I'll tan your hide."

"Gotta catch me first, Ma," the unrepentant youth jeered.

The scene tickled Irene. She laughed so hard she had to quit running. Conceding defeat, she joined Zach.

He shook his head solemnly. "What would England think?"

She pulled herself tall and managed for one instant to pull her lip straight. "At least I kept a stiff upper lip." Then she broke into gales of laughter again.

Zach, chuckling, pulled her to his side, his arm draped over her shoulder. "I'm right proud of you, Woman. You certainly know how to keep your mind on a task."

She grew serious for a moment. "I certainly do. My task today, as you said yourself, is to relax and have fun and that's exactly what I'm doing." She grinned at him, making no attempt to disguise her enjoyment—made all the more precious by his arm around her.

He stepped away. "My turn." He joined a long row of married men.

She cheered unashamedly for him as he plowed toward the finish. He didn't win. He didn't even come close for he was far too broad to contend with the slender, younger men. But that didn't matter to Irene; as far as she was concerned, there was no one else in the race. She saw only Zach.

Her gaze locked with his as he swaggered back to her side. Then she realized others were watching them, and she masked her feelings, wanting no one but Zach to see how she felt.

There were more races—the three-legged race, an egg race where partners threw a raw egg back and forth until it broke, blindfolded races, and relays. Finally, the announcer called, "Draw up teams for the tug-of-war."

The men and boys quickly drew up sides, then attached themselves to a long rope. She watched Zach join one team and saw how he skimmed the crowd until he found her. His eyes brightened, and he nodded. As he held her gaze, he spit on his palms and grabbed the rope. Only then did he free her from his intense look.

Her heart so light it felt like a butterfly, Irene cheered as Zach's team pulled the other toward them. Then when the other side prevailed, she moaned, yelling at Zach to pull. She doubted Zach could hear her above the uproar and found sweet delight in screaming his name to the sky.

Those on Zach's side must have been as stubborn as he, for ten minutes later, they pulled the opposing team to the ground.

That event seemed to mark the end of the games.

Addie, not waiting for Zach to return to their side, grabbed Irene and pulled her away. "It's time to set out the lunch."

Irene checked over her shoulder, saw Zach nod in her direction, and let herself be led away with Donald at her side. Harry had found friends and gone to play.

The table was soon covered by an abundance of food which the women had set out in order—sandwiches and pickles at one end, cakes and desserts at the other. Nearby, a barrel of water awaited the thirsty picnickers.

The announcer called for people to gather around. He asked Reverend Williams to return thanks, then lines formed to go down the table.

Zach and Harry appeared at her side.

"It looks like enough to feed an army," she whispered.

Zach looked at her long and hard. "You can't get used to how much we have, can you?"

"And to spare," she whispered. "How blessed we are."

"Amen." The word came from several directions, and Irene jerked around in surprise that so many had overheard and voiced agreement.

An older couple came up to her. "We lost our son overseas, as did many. May we never see war again." Somehow they seemed to think that because she was from England, she shared their loss. "I'm sorry," she murmured. Satisfied, they stepped back in line.

Irene filled her hands with sandwiches, as did Zach and the boys.

"We'll come back for cake," he said.

Irene grinned. "Or you could stand right here and eat."

He grinned. "I tried that one year, but Mrs. Good had her husband remove me. She said it was only fair to give everyone a chance."

"How old were you? And don't tell me it was two years ago."

"No. It was probably ten years ago. I wasn't married yet, and I thought I was a pretty sharp young fellow."

They left the table and settled on a grassy spot by themselves. She turned to him, her eyes wide with shock. "You mean you've changed your mind?"

He gave her a wide-eyed look. "I said nothing of the sort."

"Ahh. So, still thinking you're a sharp young man?" She tucked into a roast beef sandwich, suddenly very hungry.

"Of course not. No, I'm a wise, older fellow."

She almost choked on her mouthful as she chortled.

Pointedly ignoring her, he bit into a thick egg salad sandwich.

Addie and Pete and several other families joined them, and the conversation turned to other things.

They lingered over the food, enjoying the company of the others. Irene found the variety of their backgrounds fascinating and the spirit of unity heartwarming.

As soon as he finished, Harry raced off to join his friends.

Donald sat between Irene and Zach for a spell, then saw a bug a few feet away and went to investigate. Zach and Irene exchanged warm glances, acknowledging their delight in the bit of independence the move indicated.

Donald followed the bug a minute, then began collecting tiny stones into a pile.

Another little boy joined him. "Here." He handed a stone to Donald. Donald pointed at the pile. With the wordless understanding children often had, the other boy nodded and located more stones.

"Johnny!" a voice screeched.

The little boy looked up, his face contorted in alarm.

A large woman plowed toward the pair. Knowing only that she must protect Donald, Irene leapt to her feet.

The woman reached for Johnny, wrenching his arm as she jerked him to his feet. "You stay away from him. He's crazy." She glared at Irene, who stood between her and Donald. "There's something wrong with the whole family, if you ask me."

Irene drew her lips together, facing the large, angry woman without so much as a flicker of her eyelids. "Thank you very much for sharing that, but I don't remember anyone asking for your opinion." Donald huddled against her, and she pressed her hands to his shoulders. "I can't speak for anyone else here, but I for one don't care for your twisted opinion."

The woman blinked furiously, little Johnny still dangling from her grasp. "Well," she huffed, "what would you expect from someone who would marry a complete stranger?" She churned away. "Probably was the only way she could find a husband."

"I don't hear any of those concerned complaining," Irene murmured in the hollow silence.

She could feel all eyes on her but stood ramrod straight, chin high, determined no one would ever guess how the woman's words had torn at her soul.

Zach grabbed her by the shoulder and led her back to her place, keeping one arm around her. She pulled Donald into her lap, hugging him tight. "Don't ever listen to people like that," she whispered.

Addie sat on Irene's other side, her arm joining Zach's across her shoulder. "Don't you listen, either. She never says anything nice about people. Besides, she certainly doesn't speak for the rest of us."

Several murmurs of agreement acknowledged Addie's statement.

"Thank you." But Irene kept her face buried in Donald's hair, wishing she could disappear into the heavens. Or at least return to the sanctuary of home.

As if reading her thoughts, Zach leaned close and whispered, "We won't let her think she won by chasing us away."

She nodded, knowing he was right. She sat with Addie and her friends and watched the men play a game of baseball, but she had no heart for the activities and was grateful when the sun dipped toward the mountain peaks and Zach called Harry to say they were going home.

Two tired little boys settled in the back of the wagon, content to lie on their backs and watch the clouds.

Irene turned inward to her own thoughts.

Suddenly, Zach burst out laughing.

Irene shot him a startled look.

"I 'spect that's the first time anyone has stood up to Mrs. Mould."

Irene drew her lips in and turned to stare down the road, but Zach's laughter was hard to ignore.

"Boy, did you tell her off." He laughed some more.

Irene choked back her annoyance. "Is that all that matters? That someone stood up to old—what's her name? How about how I felt standing up there to be ridiculed by everyone?"

He wiped his eyes. "Not everyone," he said, his voice deep with meaning.

She looked at him, blinking before the warmth in his eyes.

He wrapped his hand over her tight fist. "Not me," he murmured, his gaze reaching into her thoughts and twisting them into a tangle.

"I know," she whispered, turning her hand to grasp his. She clung to the look in his eyes, letting him draw her into his world, into his heart.

He squeezed her hand. "I'm proud of you."

"Thank you," she whispered. Suddenly, Mrs. Mould's opinion mattered not a dash.

He seemed content to hold her hand, and she was ever so glad to let him.

The boys had fallen asleep by the time they got home. Zach carried Harry, Irene carried Donald, and they tucked them into bed without either of them stirring. Zach and Irene stood between the two cots. She ached for the right to lean back against him. Her nerves knotted when he placed his hands on her shoulders. "I think they had a good time."

She nodded, barely able to find her words. "So did I."

"Me, too." His words whispered past her ear. She could taste his breath, and she buried a moan deep inside as the ache to be in his arms choked her.

She looked down at the boys, afraid to move, wanting this moment to last forever but wanting so much more. She longed to turn into his arms. But she was afraid. What would happen if she ignored her fears and listened to her dreams? She clenched her fists, forcing courage upward. Nothing ventured. Nothing gained. She readied herself to turn. Before she could move, he stepped back, dropping his hands from her shoulders.

"I guess it's time for us to go to bed, too."

Disappointment scraped along her nerves. She took a deep breath and reminded herself of the hard things she'd faced in her life. *If I can help amputate a leg or clean gangrenous flesh, I can certainly face this man without pouring my heart out.* She forced her rigid self-control into place.

"Yes. It's about time." She waited until he strode into the kitchen before she slipped across to the bedroom and hurriedly prepared for bed.

The room had been dark for an unbearably long time before Zach entered and crawled under the covers. They lay side by side without speaking.

One thing bothered Irene. "I wish I could have stopped that woman from saying such awful things about Donald. He never misses anything. How must he feel after hearing that?"

Zach didn't answer at first. "I don't know. Just like I don't know why he's quit talking."

Irene had thought of it often. "Did something unusual happen to him?" She rushed on before he could answer. "I mean besides losing his mother?"

"Don't think so." His voice grew thick with laughter. "And now no one or nothing would dare threaten him. You'd stand up to a she bear to defend him." He chuckled. "Or Mrs. Mould, the old she-bear."

"It's not funny. Children should not have to suffer." Especially these two whom she loved so much. Her words choked past a clogged throat, ending on a sob.

"Poor Irene. Hurting for everyone else." He reached for her in the dark and pulled her into his arms.

She sniffled, letting him hold her, but not letting herself melt into his embrace, although the ache to do so consumed her insides.

"Don't worry," he murmured, his breath tickling her hair. "It will be all buttons and bows."

She giggled as he quoted her and lay her cheek against his arm.

A cry came from the other bedroom. Zach and Irene leapt to their feet and raced across the hall.

Harry sat up in bed, breathing in little gulps.

Irene dropped down beside him, Zach at her side, each wrapping their arms around him. "What's the matter?" Irene whispered.

"I had a bad dream," he gulped.

"Poor Harry," she crooned. "What was your dream about?"

He shuddered. "I kept hearing that mean lady shouting at Donald." Irene glanced at Zach, barely able to make out his eyes in the darkness. She thought Harry had been too busy playing to notice what had happened with Mrs. Mould.

"Is it true?" Harry demanded.

"What, Dear?"

"Is Donald crazy? Is he?"

"I certainly don't think so," Irene said, her anger against the woman stirring to life.

"Nor do I," Zach said.

"What do you think?" she asked Harry, then felt the tension leave his body.

"He's a man of few words."

Irene chuckled. "I'm to be quoted by all of you, aren't I?" She hugged him. "Feeling better?"

"Yes." His voice trembled.

"You go back to bed," Zach said to Irene. "I'll lay down with Harry until he settles."

She returned to a cold, lonely bed, but she couldn't be too unhappy about it. After all, Harry needed his father tonight.

The next morning, Harry trundled out to the kitchen, Donald in tow. Both boys smiled cheerily, seemingly none the worse for the events of the previous day.

Zach sidled up to her in the pretext of filling his cup with coffee. "What did I say? All buttons and bows." He gave her a smug grin.

"I'm glad." But she turned back to the stove, her thoughts troubled. If only it would be all buttons and bows for her. But every time she felt she and Zach were getting close to some sort of intimacy, they were interrupted. Perhaps Zach preferred it that way. He'd certainly never done or said anything to suggest he'd changed his mind about their marriage of convenience.

She slammed the lid on the pan unnecessarily hard. There were times she hated that phrase—marriage of convenience.

Convenience indeed. It was anything but convenient to be troubled by these longings day and night.

Lord God, she prayed silently, *help me be strong. Help me love without need for it to be returned.*

nine

Spring had blazed into summer. It seemed Zach had no sooner finished the plowing and the seeding than he announced he was taking the mower out to cut hay. Donald and Harry were instructed to stay close to the house.

"I'll be in the garden," Irene said. "There's a mat of weeds like a carpet out there. I could use a couple of boys to help."

And so she set them digging between the potatoes while she hoed and picked along the rows. She straightened, arching her back to ease the kinks. The sun sucked at the ground, so bright it hurt her eyes and so hot the sweat rolled down her back. "Let's get a cool drink," she called to the boys. They had long since grown tired of pulling weeds and settled down to play in a shady corner. "Are you building another farm?" It seemed one of their favorite activities.

Harry scrambled to his feet. "Maybe we should take Dad a drink."

"That's a good idea. The water he took with him will be warm by now."

A few minutes later they walked past a wheat field, now green and lush, toward the field where Zach cut hay. The grass lay in a neat, flat carpet. Irene breathed deeply.

Zach saw them coming and left the mower. "Am I glad to see you," he called, wiping his face on his sleeve as he headed their direction. "It's a hot one today." He downed the water in large gulps. "Thank you." His eyes reflected back the warmth of the bright sun.

Irene held his gaze for a moment. Since the day of the picnic, she'd detected a change in his attitude toward her. It seemed he smiled more readily and met her eyes often, holding her gaze until she felt as if their souls were being forged into one. But what made her thoughts rattle about in her head like the boys had thrown in a handful of marbles was the way he casually dropped a hand to her arm or draped an arm around her shoulders.

"If I get this up dry, we'll have plenty of feed for the winter."

"How much more do you have to cut?" She looked out over the hay field. How quickly she'd learned the farming routines. Almost as amazing as how quickly and thoroughly she'd fallen in love with him.

"I should finish cutting tonight." He picked up a handful from the swath at their feet, squeezed it, then sniffed it. "I'll be able to start racking right away. See." He shoved the handful of hay toward her. "Smell it." Avoiding his eyes lest he guess her thoughts had been on him, she buried her nose in the fragrant grasses. "See how dry it is." She squeezed it as she had seen him do, her fingers catching on his rough palm.

He closed his hand around her fist. Startled, she lifted her face and met his luminous look. Her heart tripped into a race. Certain her eyes would give her away, she tried to pull away, but she was trapped. For the life of her, she could not tear her gaze from his. "It is as you said one day, we are truly blessed."

She could not remember ever saying such, but she would have agreed with anything he said at that moment. "We certainly are," she murmured, hoping her words didn't sound as breathless as they felt.

"You have a bit of hay in your hair."

She closed her eyes as he plucked something from above her right eye. The urge to turn her face into his palm and kiss it was so strong she groaned, not certain if she had been successful in restricting the sound to her insides.

His hand moved.

Her heart forgot to beat as she caught her breath and waited, but he only picked another blade of grass from behind her ear before he released his grasp on her hand and tossed the handful of hay on the ground.

"Got to make hay while the sun shines," he muttered and strode back to the patient horse.

Irene grabbed up the jar of water and fled back to the house with the boys on her heels. She spent the afternoon tenaciously weeding under the hot sun, hoping the heat and discomfort would absolve her of a desperate longing for something more real from Zach.

&

Zach finished the mowing and turned to racking. The long hours he put in away from the house provided Irene with a measure of relief from her errant emotions.

Then he had to haul the hay home in a rack.

"Harry can come and drive the horse while I fork up the hay."

Harry smiled so wide his eyes turned upward at the corners. "I get to help?" And when Zach said, "yes," Harry's chest swelled.

Irene studied the pleased boy. "You've been helping all the time, Harry."

He grew serious. "Yes, but this is man's work."

Irene laughed. "I see. Of course that makes a vast difference."

He nodded. "I get to drive the horse."

"So I understand. Have you done so before?"

"Dad let me drive lots of times, didn't you, Dad?"

"A time or two, Son." Seeing the disappointment on Harry's face, he added, "But you did just fine. I know you can handle it."

Harry strode out after his father, trying desperately to match his steps. Irene smiled.

Zach took Harry with him several days after that.

The weather changed abruptly, heavy clouds building over the mountains, a gray, cold wind shivering down the valley.

Frowning, Zach studied the sky. "I hope I can beat the storm."

Harry rose from the supper table. "Not tonight, Son. I'll manage without you."

Irene studied Zach's face, wondering why he'd instructed Harry to remain at home this evening when he was under pressure to finish.

Zach returned her look and muttered, "He's put in a long day already. I don't want to push the boy."

She nodded agreement. Harry seemed content to play with Donald after supper, and Irene settled down with some mending. She checked the sky often. As long as the clouds clung to the mountaintops, the storm would stay in the distance; but if the clouds hurried close, they could expect a drenching.

A black cloud darkened the room. Lightning rent the skies. Thunder rolled down the valley.

"Is it going to storm?" Harry asked.

"It's a long ways off yet. I'm sure your dad will be home before it gets this far." Lightning danced back and forth; the noise of empty barrels rolling across the sky echoed through the room.

A different noise filled the room. Harry's eyes grew round as saucers; Donald's face filled with fear. "What was that?"

Irene shuddered. "I'm not sure."

It came again, shrill, screeching over her nerves. Then Zach's distant roar. "Whoa!"

Irene was on her feet like a bolt of lightning. She caught Harry before he reached the kitchen door. "You stay with Donald. Whatever you do, don't leave the house." She grabbed a coat with one hand and wrenched the door open with the other, bounding into the flashing night toward the hay field.

Again Zach's voice called, "Settle down."

In the blinding flashes, she saw the horse rearing, Zach at his head, trying to pull him down. Her mouth dry with the taste of fear, she raced to Zach's side and grabbed the halter.

"What are you doing here?" Zach demanded, his voice hoarse. "Where are the boys?"

"They're safe. What do you want me to do?" Another bolt of lightning sent the huge horse into a frenzy. It was all the both of them could do to hold him. His plate-sized front hooves flailed in the air, inches from the humans who did their best to calm him.

Through clenched teeth, Zach grunted, "This is no place for you."

In the next flash of light, she saw his angry eyes, but she only smiled and said, "What do we need to do?"

For a moment more, he stared at her, then the horse neighed—a sharp, panic-laced sound—and Zach turned to the animal. "Whoa, there boy." He spoke to Irene in the same tone of voice. "If you can hold him a minute, I'll unhitch him. Whoa, Matt. That's the boy. Settle down now. I don't think there's any point in trying to get the rack in tonight. Whoa. That's a boy. Let me unbuckle you."

Lightning flashed again, brighter, closer and Matt rolled his eyes, shuddering under Irene's hand. "Be careful," she whispered, but the thunder drowned out her words.

Finally, the horse was freed, and Zach grabbed the head strap and led him toward the barn. Matt strained against his hand, but Zach shook his arm. "Settle down now."

Irene retained her hold on the horse, trotting at his side as they crossed the field.

Zach continued muttering. Irene realized his words were directed at her. "This is no place for a woman. It's not woman's work."

Stung by his reaction, Irene spoke her mind clearly. "The war made men out of a lot of women."

Zach pushed the barn door open with his free hand and led the horse inside. Irene quickly stepped aside and let Zach deal with the animal as she tried to calm her thoughts. She would not argue with Zach.

But her good intentions fled as he put the horse in a stall, then spun to face her. "The war is over."

She glared at him. "I'm well aware of that. But I didn't need the war to convince me I'm no namby-pamby." Her chest heaved, partly from the exertion of getting Matt to the barn, but more so from the anger and frustration building like a swelling tide.

He leaned forward, almost nose to nose with her, but she

refused to back up. "You got no sense, either."

She pressed closer. Close enough to see the dark emotion raging in him. She could practically smell his anger. "I expect you're right. That would explain why I'm here."

He drew in a sharp breath. "I knew the time would come you'd throw it back in my face."

She'd gone too far, but her anger was out of control. "This isn't about me. Or what constitutes a woman's place. This is about how different I am from Esther. I don't think you'll ever accept me for who I am. All you want is someone who is another Esther." She spun on her heel and marched away. She could hear him slam something against the wall before thunder blocked out all other sound.

She paused halfway to the house, letting the wind tear at her hair, striving to regain her self-control. She looked toward the spot where she could see the mountains on a sunny day and uttered a desperate prayer. "God, I fail and fail. It's because I want so much more than I can hope for. But could You please let him love me just a little? Or else teach me to be patient and content with what I have. I have lots, Lord. I know that, and I don't mean to be ungrateful. Just give me strength."

Cold splatters danced across her skin. And reason returned.

"What have I done?" she moaned. "He will never forgive me for that outburst." Her shoulders slumped as she crossed to the house.

Rain pounded against the house before Zach returned, water dripping from his nose and chin. He avoided her eyes as she handed him a towel.

Clutching at her stomach to still the sudden lurching as she realized how much his rejection hurt, she turned and gasped. Zach's pants were torn, a steady stream of blood flowed into his sock.

"You're hurt."

"It's nothing." He half turned away.

"Daddy, you're bleeding," Harry wailed. Donald's eyes reflected the darkness of the outside.

"It's nothing," Zach growled. "A little cut."

"It doesn't look little to me." Irene stood closer to examine it.

"I'm fine." He spat the words out.

"We'll know after I have a good look at it." She faced him, her hands on her hips. "Into the bedroom with you." She reached for a basin of water and some clean cloths. "Harry, you keep Donald here until I've cleaned it up; then you can come in. I'll call you."

Zach held his ground.

She faced him unblinking and firm. "Come along," she urged. "Or can't you walk?"

"I can walk," he muttered, stomping into the bedroom.

She followed, ignoring his glare as he turned on his heel.

"Remove your trousers," she ordered as she pushed the door closed with her elbow.

"I beg your pardon."

"Oh, come on. You sleep beside me every night with them off." His jaw set into a hard line, and he refused to budge.

"Besides, did you forget I'm a nurse? I've seen many a man with his pants down."

"I'm sure you have," he muttered.

She ignored his jibe. "Or I can cut them off." Silently, they faced each other. She knew she had to win this fight for the sake of his wound. And yes, she admitted, for her own sake.

She knew the moment he gave in. He sighed with annoyance.

"Did you ever bend your will to anyone?"

Pretending he meant as a nurse with her patients, she smiled sweetly. "I managed to persuade them one way or another."

"I can imagine." He slipped his trousers down and sat on the edge of the bed.

"All the way," she ordered.

Grumbling under his breath, he kicked the trousers aside.

"Lie down."

He began to protest, then grunted and lifted his feet to the bed and stretched out, his arms crossed over his chest. "Woman, you are a bother."

She covered him with a quilt and turned to the injury, sponging at it gently. "It's a nasty gash, but I don't think I'll have to sew it up."

"What?" He half sat.

She pushed him back, laughing low in her throat. "I'm only joking."

He darted an annoyed look at her and fell back so she could finish cleaning the wound.

"I'm sorry about earlier," she murmured, finding it easier to broach the subject while she had an excuse to avoid eye contact. "I didn't mean to sound like I regretted being here." She spent a great deal of effort on cleansing the wound. "I don't regret it for a moment."

She held her breath waiting for his response—not daring to look at him.

She jumped nervously when his hand touched her shoulder and turned her to face him.

"Are you sure?" His gaze bored into her, dark, demanding, searching. "Not anything?"

She blinked hard, determined not to let him guess just how much she loved him. "I regret nothing. If I could do it again, I would do the same thing."

He pulled her closer, drawing her alongside the bed until she was inches from his face. Her heart ticked loudly.

His warm breath, tasting slightly of supper's coffee and the cool storm outside, tickled at her lashes. The yearning inside her swelled into a mighty roar. Her jaw quivered as he drew her close.

Sure he was going to kiss her, she leaned toward him.

"Is Daddy all right?" Harry's worried voice sliced through the moment.

Zach fell back against the bed. Irene withdrew, pressing her hands together in her lap.

"He's fine," she murmured. "He'll be out in a minute, as soon as I put on a dressing."

She glanced at Zach, seeing a reflection of her own frustration in the tightness of his jaw.

She dressed the wound and left so Zach could pull on clean trousers. Her nerves tingled like lightning had come too close.

She heard him enter the room but kept her back to him. The boys exclaimed over him and demanded attention. He took them to the front room and read to them. Life settled back to normal.

After the boys were tucked in, Zach stood looking out the window. "The storm is over. It looks as calm as glass out there." He paused. "Do you want to go for a walk?"

Her cup rattled in the saucer, and she shoved it away, clenching her hands in her lap, wondering as to his intent. Was he thinking of what had happened in the bedroom? Did he plan to continue what he'd begun? Did she want him to? Her knuckles grew white as she squeezed her hands together. Yes, she wanted him to kiss her. To love her. Just as she was—bigger than Esther, inclined to be independent, and sometimes boisterous with the joy of life.

"I'd like that," she said, her voice surprisingly calm.

He waited as she pulled on a coat. He stuffed his hands in the pockets of his own coat as he set his stride to match hers.

The air tasted of rain and thunder. Moisture clung to every blade and leaf, glistening silver in the moonlight.

They walked to the end of the yard, neither speaking. Irene let the peace of the evening soothe her bristled nerves.

They paused near some trees, listening to the drip of water from the leaves. Zach took her hand and turned her to face him. "Irene, I . . ." He broke off, examining her face. "You got yourself into a real mess when you married me."

"No, Zach. I didn't." She smiled at him. "I got myself a family I love." She hoped he would respond to her barely concealed admission.

He studied her closely, but he didn't say the words she longed for. Instead, he pulled her close and tipped his head to give her a sweet, gentle kiss. It was as short as it was sweet. She stared at him, knowing her eyes were as wide as young Donald's often were.

"Don't look so surprised," he murmured.

"Well, I am." Surprised and confused. What did it mean?

"Come on, we better get back." Taking her hand, he led her back to the house. "Time for bed," he said after they'd removed their coats.

She hesitated. Had their situation changed? But he sat at the table and pulled out his jackknife to clean his nails. She turned toward the bedroom, the emptiness inside her greater than she'd ever known before.

She hurried under the covers, pausing to read her Bible. "Lord," she prayed, "help Zach to love me, and if he can't, help me be strong and kind and true." Her heart calmer, she turned out the lantern and waited. In the moonlight, the leaves outside the window were silver shadows. The damp air carried the scent of wild roses. A cloud covered the moon, deepening the darkness. Still, Zach did not come.

She scrubbed the heel of her hand across her eyes. Had Zach been testing to see how much he liked her? Having kissed her, was he still convinced to leave things as they were? She pressed her hands into her eyes. She would not cry. There was no point in it. She reminded herself of her words to Zach. *I regret nothing. I've got a family to love.* She would do it again if she had the choice. There was only one thing she would change. She wanted, more than anything, for Zach to love her. But it seemed his memories were too fresh, too dear for him to let them go. But that didn't stop her from loving him. She would continue to love them all with her whole heart.

❧

"You're coming with me to the ladies' tea," Addie insisted. "Everyone will be there."

Irene refrained from saying that, alone, was reason enough not to go.

Addie appealed to her brother. "Zach, you tell her she should go."

Zach snorted. "Irene does what she likes."

Irene stared at Zach, uncertain if he meant it as a compliment or criticism.

He gave her a slow smile. "Suit yourself, Irene."

Slow warmth crept up her limbs and curled inside her. He didn't seem to mind letting her do as she wished. Suddenly, an outing with Addie seemed a fine way to spend an afternoon.

And so, a bit later, she sat beside Addie on the buggy seat. "Where exactly are we going?"

"To the home of Mr. and Mrs. Goodyear. They own a large house with wonderful flowers and lawns. For several years, Mrs. Goodyear has invited the ladies of the area to come for tea. She serves all sorts of nice fancies and tubs of tea and everyone has a lovely visit."

Irene settled back. "It sounds fun."

"It is. No menfolk and no children but the littlest. For awhile, we all feel like real ladies."

Irene laughed. "Nobody would think I was a lady if they'd seen me this week."

Addie slanted her a look. "What did that brother of mine have you up to?"

"Oh, it wasn't him." She shook her head. "In fact he was quite perturbed when he found out."

"Well, I'm dying of curiosity. What were you doing?"

"I decided to give the stove a good cleaning."

"That sounds normal enough."

"It was until I tried to clean the dust off the stovepipes." She chuckled. "I guess I got too enthusiastic. I brought a length of pipe down." Black soot had billowed all over her, settling over the kitchen like some sort of disease. "Great," she'd murmured. "Wonderful." Thankfully, the boys were outside, and Zach was out in the field. "Now I have to scrub everything." But first she'd had to heat water, which she couldn't do until she put the pipe back up.

"I might as well clean them all," she'd muttered. With a great deal of tugging and grunting, she'd managed to disconnect several lengths of pipe and took them outside to clean, hoping she'd be able to put everything back together.

"You never mentioned you were also a chimney sweep." A deep, amused voice had spoken so close to her she'd jerked up, dropping the length of pipe with a clatter and a choking cloud of black soot.

"Don't be sneaking up on me like that," she'd muttered when she'd finished coughing.

"Bad day?" he'd asked, grinning.

"No. It's a fine day. Look around you. Isn't the sun bright and the sky fair? It's a dandy fine day all round."

He'd chuckled with frank amusement. "Have you looked at yourself in the mirror lately?"

She'd wrinkled her nose and held up her hands. "I'm black as the inside of a barrel, but I can't wash until I can start a fire again."

"What are you trying to do?" he asked as he strode to the kitchen.

"I'm trying to clean the place." Her annoyance had mounted with each of his words. "I don't need someone standing around mocking me while I do it."

He'd stared at her like she'd suddenly sprung two heads. "What possessed you to clean the pipes by yourself? And how, pray tell, do you expect to get back in place?"

"I didn't plan. . . ." What was the use in trying to explain? "I thought perhaps some kind. . ." She'd lingered on the word. "Gentleman would offer to help."

He'd stared at her so long she finally grunted and turned back to trying to assemble the pipes.

"You'll never get it that way." He'd then carried the pipes inside. "Here, hold this in place."

She'd done as instructed.

"You can be the most perverse woman sometimes," he'd muttered.

Too hot and dirty to care what he thought, she'd simply handed him the last section of pipe and stood back while he tightened the strapping to hold it in place.

He'd faced her, his expression as sour as the milk she'd thrown to the chickens yesterday. "Next time, perhaps you wouldn't mind consulting me before you try to fix the stove or move a wall or build a fireplace or whatever harebrained ideas might be brewing in that mind of yours." And he strode from the room.

Stung into silence, she'd stared after him. "Harebrained?" She'd never been called that before. She'd raced to the door. "I'll have you know I was at the top of my class when I graduated. Besides. . ." Her voice had dropped a note. "It was an accident."

He'd ground to a halt, turning slowly. "How could it be an accident you graduated at the top of your class?"

"Knocking down the stovepipe was an accident."

He'd gaped at her. "Then why did you let me go on like I did?"

She'd glowered. "How was I to stop you?"

"I guess I sort of ran off at the mouth, didn't I?" He'd stepped closer.

She'd shrugged. "Far be it from me to judge."

"It's awful hard to take you serious when your cheeks are all blackened and your eyes stick out like that." Then he'd chuckled.

"I'm glad I can offer you some amusement." And suddenly, she'd started laughing. "I've got to clean up the mess in the kitchen."

"Do you want some help?" he'd asked with a chuckle.

Addie shifted around to stare at her. "And did he help you?"

Irene nodded. "We scrubbed all afternoon. It was a lot of work," she added when Addie looked thoughtful.

"Zach helped wash the kitchen?" Addie sounded confused. "Yes, why?"

Addie shrugged. "He's always been such a stickler for woman's work and men's work and never the twain shall meet, if you know what I mean."

Irene lifted her hands in resignation. "I suppose the lines lessened when he had to be both mother and father to the

boys." She refrained from saying anything about the dis-
agreements they had when she pushed the lines even more.

The conversation ended as they arrived at their destination.

Mrs. Goodyear had set tables and chairs on the lawn, each
table with a crisp linen cloth. A longer table stood in front of
the house with a magnificent silver tea set and rows of fine
china teacups. Cloths covered plates that Irene supposed
were filled with the dainties Addie had mentioned.

"It's like home," Irene whispered, choking back a flood
of tears.

"Do you miss it very much?" Addie asked.

"Not often, but sometimes something will hit me. Like
this." Addie waited as Irene pressed back tears. "But life is
too full to waste time pining. I'll get back to visit someday,
I'm sure. And Grace is close enough to visit occasionally."
She grabbed Addie's arm. "Come on, let's go join the fun."

A regal lady with a wide-brimmed straw hat and a long
silk dress in pale green oversaw the garden party. Irene soon
discovered that part of the program included circulating from
group to group, visiting awhile before moving on.

Irene moved to a new table, Addie by now on the far side
of the yard. For a moment, Irene was alone, waiting for others
to join her.

"No one knows for sure, of course, but it seems reasonable to
assume that the poor dear just quit living." The whispered voice
reached Irene from behind the tiny rose arbor where another
table nestled. She couldn't help overhearing the conversation.

"I heard she was never strong."

"Yes, I heard that, too. But can you imagine what those two
boys went through? No wonder the little one stopped talking."

Irene's head came up with a snap. Were they talking about
Donald and Harry? And Esther? She kept still, hoping to
catch the rest of the conversation.

"You know, I heard she was dead several days before anyone found her."

"No!"

Irene's stomach churned. She stumbled to her feet, looking around blindly for an escape, and found shelter beside a low shed. She pressed her hand to her chest, trying to control her ragged breathing. Could it be true? Had the boys been in the house with their dead mother? She shuddered. It was too awful to contemplate.

Slowly, her breathing settled; her heartbeat returned to normal. She smoothed her expression. No one would guess she felt like someone had poured a bucket of slop into her insides.

The rest of the afternoon passed agonizingly slowly.

On the way home, she turned to Addie. "What happened to Esther?"

Addie gave her a wary look. "What has Zach said?"

"Nothing, but you must tell me. I have to know what happened."

"Why are you suddenly so interested?"

Irene grabbed Addie's arm. "I've always thought she was ill. I don't know what I thought, but I must know."

"Did someone say something to you?"

"I overheard some comments."

Addie sighed. "People have said all sorts of things." She drove on without speaking. Irene squeezed her arm again. Addie nodded. "I'll tell you what I know. Perhaps she was sick before Zach left. If she was, she hid it, but after he joined the army, she got weaker and weaker. I thought at first she was having trouble adjusting and given a little time. . ." She rubbed her forehead as if trying to scrub away the memories.

"Pete and I tried to get over as often as we could, but we had so many things to look after with moving into our own home and his brother being sent home injured and all. When we finally got over, we found Esther in bed, too weak to care for the boys. We took her and the boys home, but she never recovered."

A shiver reached up Irene's spine and shook her shoulders. "What about the boys?" Her throat was so tight she could barely speak.

Addie placed her hand over Irene's. "They were huddled together in their room, almost too afraid to move."

Silence settled heavily over them.

Finally, in an agonized voice, Irene whispered, "Those poor boys."

ten

The house was empty when Addie dropped Irene off. "Thanks for the good afternoon."

Addie gave her a sad look. "I didn't mean to upset you. Try to forget about it."

Irene nodded and waved as Addie gave the reins a flick and headed out of the yard.

Irene stumbled inside. Her pain practically drove her to her knees. What had her poor little boys been through? How much had they seen? Worse, how much had they imagined? She hadn't truly cried for years—not since her own mother died. But hot tears would not be contained and spilled down her cheeks. She grabbed the kitchen towel, pressing her face into it to stem the flood.

"Forget about it," Addie had said. But Irene knew that wasn't the answer. Too much had been buried, too many things left unsaid. All she could do was pray for healing for this family and pray God would use her and help her bridle her tongue. Her greatest fear was she'd do harm rather than good.

By the time Zach came thumping in, two little boys hurrying after him, Irene had dried her tears and washed her face. Her mind was made up to confront Zach with her discovery.

She waited until he crawled into bed beside her in the dark.

"How was your afternoon?" he asked.

"Very fine. A real nice time for all the ladies."

"Hmm. Not my cup of tea."

She chuckled at his choice of words, then grew serious. "Seems it's the time to share all the news of the community."

He grunted. "No doubt. Probably half of it made up."

Her well-rehearsed words seemed suddenly flat in view of his perceptive analysis of a bunch of women together. "I'm certain there's some truth in what you say, just as there is often some truth in peoples' speculations."

She hoped he would take the bait.

"I get the feeling you're referring to something more than idle chatter." He sounded on edge.

"I suppose I am." She suddenly wished she could be spared this whole scene. "I overheard a conversation. I believe they were talking about Esther and the boys."

He made a noise in his chest that could have been agreement.

"They said things I need to have clarified."

He remained silent.

"Please tell me the circumstances of Esther's death?"

She lay quietly at his side, willing him to answer her question, even though she guessed by the way he stiffened that he was displeased by it.

"What's there to say? I guess she got sick, and with no one to care for her, it was too much."

She waited, praying he would go on.

"I didn't know until it was too late." His voice, crackling with pain, tore at her heart. She wanted to reach for him, assure him of her love and understanding, but she sensed how brittle his feelings were and wondered if he was angry with her for bringing up Esther's death. "There was nothing I could do." Someone else hearing his flat tone of voice might have thought he showed little emotions, but Irene knew how much self-control lay quivering under those emotionless words.

"I'm sorry, Zach."

"Don't be sorry for me. Be sorry for Esther."

She blinked. He wasn't making sense. "What do you mean, be sorry for Esther?"

"Figure it out yourself. She was the one left alone to deal with all the responsibilities. To lay in bed so sick she couldn't help herself and have no one to do for her. I deserve whatever suffering I have to endure. She didn't."

"Are you saying you're to blame?"

Angry now, he ground the words out. "Yes, I'm to blame."

She hated the self-loathing and despair she heard in his voice. "How are you to blame?" she demanded. "Are you God, to be responsible for life and death?"

"Not God. Her husband. She was my first responsibility. But I couldn't see that. All I could see was my need to play hero and join the army. And what did it gain me? The war ended without me. I lost everything."

"And how were you supposed to know she would get sick? Hundreds of men left their families behind without any more assurances than you had. Why should you blame yourself for what happened?"

"Who do you suggest I blame? No one forced me to go. In fact, Esther begged me not to, but I wouldn't listen."

"What about the boys?"

"What about them?" His hoarse tone warned her he didn't want to discuss the boys.

But she forged on, knowing there were things that had to be said. "What happened to the boys?"

The harsh sound of his breathing was his only answer.

She pushed aside the swell of tears clogging her throat, promising herself she would not cry. "What did our poor little boys see during those weeks? What did they think? Has anyone ever talked to them about it to see what happened? How they feel?" She broke off, her voice cracking.

"It's best to forget about the past and get on with the present."

"The present rides on the back of the past," she protested, but Zach flung to his side, practically falling off the bed, he clung so tight to the edge. Irene knew nothing she said at this point would make any difference.

The next morning, he studiously avoided meeting her gaze and sat staring morosely into his coffee cup. She carried the coffeepot to him, touching his shoulder as she offered more.

He jerked away like she'd slapped him.

The pot quivered in her hand, then she pushed her shoulders back and silently filled his cup.

The boys came from their bedroom.

"Can we go with you again today?" Harry asked.

Zach shook his head without looking up. "Not today, Son. You stay with your mama."

The way Harry's face crumpled before he sighed in resignation, his expression serious and controlled, widened the cracks in Irene's heart. She hurried to set the pot on the back of the stove and clenched her hands together. She hadn't meant for the children to be hurt again. She almost wished she could take back the questions she'd raised last night. But her study of medicine made her certain that covering an infection with a clean dressing was futile. The wound had to be cleansed. And this family had a wound that needed to be cleansed. So if God chose to use her for their healing, to bring peace to them, she would gladly bear whatever pain it brought to her own heart.

She kept her back to the room, praying for strength and wisdom. By the time she turned, her inner peace had been restored, and she was able to smile as she asked Harry, "Isn't this the day we decided to find a rosebush to plant on the hillside?" She'd talked to the boys about her desire to plant a bush or two where the wash water ran down the hill. "No point in wasting the water," she'd said, "when we could enjoy seeing something benefit from it."

Harry rewarded her with a smile that sent sparks into his eyes. "Are we going to get one ten feet tall?"

She laughed, her humor restored. "Maybe we better find something smaller to dig up." She squeezed his upper arm. "I'm not sure you're strong enough to carry a ten-foot bush."

He flexed his arm and studied the swelling at his biceps. "I'm pretty strong, right, Dad?"

"Yes, Son." But his gaze didn't touch the boy.

"Someday I'll be as strong as my dad," Harry bragged.

Irene nodded. "I'm sure you will."

As soon as they'd finished eating, the boys rushed to help Irene with the dishes. "We gotta go bush hunting," Harry told Donald. Donald nodded, his black eyes dancing with pleasure.

Zach slapped his hat on his head and left, mumbling something about work to do.

Irene couldn't believe how much it hurt to see him turn inward on himself, shutting her out completely—and even the boys to a lesser extent. A few months ago, no one could have made her believe how intricately woven she would become with Zach and the boys, so much so that their pain was her pain, and rejection the sharpest arrow of all.

"I'll get a spade," Harry offered, racing to the barn to find one.

They wandered along the road, armed with shovel, gloves, and a gunnysack, searching the fence line for the most colorful and fragrant rosebush. The sweetness of the wild roses tore at her insides. *Love should be like that, sweet and pure.* She picked a fragile blossom, pricking her finger on a thorn and grimaced. Perhaps love was more like wild roses than she'd realized, full of sweetness when in full bloom, fragile as the soft petals that fell to the ground at her touch, and studded with thorns to tear at one's flesh.

"We'll take this one." She pointed to the one on which she'd pricked her finger. "And this." In the end, they carried home half a dozen roots and dug them into the brow of the hill.

"How big will they grow?" Harry demanded, still stuck on her tales of ten-foot bushes.

"You saw them along the road. I suppose they'll grow that tall." *If they survive the move,* she added to herself, struck again by the parallel to her own life. Her love would thrive if Zach could survive the loss of his first wife, but today, for the first time since she'd married him, she wondered if he would, instead, wither and die inside.

After they'd cleaned up the tools, the boys went to play with their farm of twigs and marbles. She watched them. Donald still sucked on his fingers; Harry remained, for the most part, far too serious. She was convinced they hid secrets in their little minds, memories of their mother's death that chained them to that event. She was equally convinced they could not break free from those chains until they were given the freedom and encouragement to discuss what had happened.

As the boys played, she went inside and knelt by her bed, praying for God's wisdom and strength in dealing with this issue. Her first instinct was to demand Zach face the issue and deal with it, but she knew she couldn't force her will on him. Only God could help him confront his past.

❧

Day after day, Zach remained morose and withdrawn. She saw the boys lose much of the ground they'd gained since she'd come, and she knew the issue must be faced. But she put it off, fearing Zach's reaction. She admitted she couldn't bear the thought of driving him further from her.

Night was the worst time. Over the summer they'd achieved an easiness that made it possible to touch in the night, knowing the other wouldn't jump away in alarm. But now Irene could have stuffed both boys between them with ease. And if they happened to inadvertently touch, Zach practically jumped out of bed.

She didn't know how she would deal with any more distance between them. She smiled thinking if Zach added any more distance between them in bed, he would end up on the floor.

Yet it was not a situation that invited humor. Her nerves were taut from the strain. She knew the boys felt it as well.

Finally, she came to a decision. She could put off facing Zach no longer.

Before Zach could push to his feet after dinner the next day, Irene said, "I need to talk to you." The boys had gone out to play so it was an ideal time.

He gave her a sharp look. "So go ahead. Speak your piece."

Her courage almost abandoned her. She took a deep breath, clenching her hands together in her lap. "We need to talk to the boys about their mother's death. You need to talk to them."

He glowered at her, his eyes dark with anger. "Why can't you let things alone? I don't see the need for stirring things up."

Her eyes burned from forcing herself to meet his gaze without blinking. "They deserve a chance to express themselves."

"There's no need for them to face the pain again." He turned away, dismissing her request.

She pressed her lips into a tight line and reached deep inside herself for strength. "You mean you can't face the pain again. Look at your sons and tell me they don't face it every day."

A flash of agony crossed his face, tearing at her heart like barbs from the rosebushes outside the door. "What do you expect?" He buried his face in his hands. "I should have seen it coming."

"Oh no, it isn't your fault." She sprang to his side, kneeling beside him, urgently grasping his knees. "How can you blame yourself? How were you to know she would get sick? You're putting far too much on yourself."

He jerked to his feet, pushing her aside.

She scrambled to her feet, an ache thudding behind her eyeballs, a spasm of pain clenching at her neck.

"That's easy for you to say." His words were so taut they came out as a groan. "You seem to have all the answers except one. How do I forget? How do I forgive myself?" He strode from the house like a man trying to escape the pursuit of ghosts.

Irene stared after him, knowing he fled his own ghosts—ghosts of his own making, but nevertheless, ones that must be conquered before he could be whole again. Before he could offer her love.

Perhaps he would never be able to love her. Even so, she wished to see him freed from this torture.

He returned for supper but sat hunched over his plate, his fists curled into knots beside the plate. After toying with his food for a few minutes, he shoved his chair back, the sound echoing like a gunshot. "I've things to do," he muttered and strode from the house.

Two boys stared at him. Donald sucked his fingers, his eyes round and black. Harry's expression was shuttered, his eyes wary. "Where's Dad going?" he asked.

Irene tried to lighten the mood. "He must have something he needs to do. He'll be back soon." Her heart heavy with the weight of their strained looks, she asked, "Who wants to play hide-and-seek after we do dishes?"

"I guess not." Harry carried his dishes to the counter. "Maybe we'll play with our blocks."

"That's fine." She realized they were even more troubled by Zach's behavior than she'd guessed.

She let the boys play long past bedtime, hoping Zach would return to put them to bed. Their glances slid often toward the door, and they strained toward every noise even as she did.

"Boys, it's time to get ready for bed," she announced when she could delay it no longer.

"Dad's not home yet," Harry said.

"I know, but he'll be back when he's finished whatever he's doing. He would expect you to go to bed."

Harry and Donald exchanged looks, then Harry nodded. "I guess so."

She read to them a few minutes even though she guessed they weren't listening, just as she knew they weren't sleeping when they closed their eyes and lay still. She pressed a kiss to each forehead and murmured, "Go to sleep, boys."

In the kitchen, she stared out the window. The August evening still held enough light to see down the trail. Several times she thought she saw an approaching figure on horseback, but it was only the shifting shadow of a tree.

She shivered, shadows filling her mind and soul as she prepared for bed. She opened her Bible, but the words danced meaninglessly before her eyes. After a moment, she gave up and closed the pages. "Oh, God," she cried, "where is he? What is he doing? Lord, work in his heart. Please, please bring him home safely."

She lay in the gloom of the half dark, her eyes wide and hollow. At a noise outside the window, she jerked to her feet and dashed to the door. But it was only a tree branch shifting in the dark. She crawled back under the covers, shivering despite the warm air. When another sound startled along her nerves, she pulled the covers over her head and forced her eyes closed.

The sun blared through the window, already well up in the sky when Irene sat up, instantly awake. Zach was not in bed. She dashed from the room. He was not in the kitchen. She skidded into the front room. It echoed with emptiness. She trudged back to the bedroom and dressed.

She made coffee as usual and prepared breakfast, all the time wondering what had happened to Zach. All sorts of visions filled her mind—Zach lying injured on the road, Zach bloodied and hurting after a bear attack. She squeezed her eyes tight, trying to block out the pictures and prayed God's protection on Zach. "And bring him back safely," she murmured.

"Where's Dad?" Harry demanded.

She turned slowly, smoothing her expression. "He's not here."

"Didn't he come home?" Two pairs of eyes bored into her, demanding the truth, begging for reassurance.

"No, he didn't."

Harry's face crumpled. "He's gone. He's gone, too. No one wants to stay with us." He sobbed in little gasps as Donald's eyes grew rounder and the sucking noises stronger.

Irene rushed to the children and pulled them into her arms. "That's not true. Your dad will be back, I promise."

Harry clung to her. "For sure?"

"He will always come back. He loves you."

Harry nodded into her shoulder. "He came back from the war even though Mommy said he wouldn't."

Irene closed her eyes against the pain. How could a mother fill her child's mind with such terrors? "Besides, now you've got me. In fact, you're stuck with me. I won't be leaving even if you get tired of my funny face and my English accent."

Harry leaned back to smile at her and touched her face. "You have a nice face."

"Thank you." She squeezed the words past the lump in her throat.

"And I like the way you talk."

She hugged him close, too overwhelmed to speak. This dear little boy was worth whatever pain her love for Zach caused her. She edged back to a chair, pulling Donald to her lap.

"We won't get tired of you," Harry murmured, resting against her shoulder.

"And I will never get tired of you."

They hugged together, the warm little bodies bringing comfort to her tortured soul.

They were still huddled together when the door opened, and Zach stepped in.

Irene jerked her head up, her heart pounding with alarm at his sudden appearance.

Harry flew from her arms, launching himself at his father. "Dad, Dad, where were you? She said you'd be back."

Irene set Donald down so he could run to his father.

Zach hugged Harry and scooped Donald into his arms. His gaze skidded past Irene. "I'll have a cup of coffee, please."

The boys were content to have their father back without explanation and tucked into their breakfast with hearty appetites.

Irene could not so easily forget his absence and poked at her food.

Zach ate slowly and steadily, pushing his plate away when he finished. He downed the last of his coffee, then stood. "Harry, come help me with the chores." And he left without a word of explanation or apology.

Irene stared after him, her thoughts hopelessly tangled.

eleven

She waited until the milk had been strained and set to cool before she spoke quietly to Harry. "Take Donald outside to play for awhile." Harry gave her a questioning look, then seeing her little nod, took Donald and led him away.

Zach headed toward the door, but she blocked his escape, facing him squarely. "I wanted to be able to help you and the boys." Her chest ached so hard it hurt to speak, but she forged ahead, ignoring the pain. "I wanted to live up to my name; Irene, bringer of peace."

He faced her, arms at his sides, a cautious look on his face.

She continued past the tightness in her throat. "Instead, I've driven you away. Away from your own home. I'm sorry." She caught her bottom lip in her teeth, her nose stinging with unshed tears, but she was past the point of caring whether her eyes glittered, giving away the depth of her emotion.

He drew his mouth back, trying to smile. "I know. You promised all buttons and bows, and it hasn't worked out that way, has it?"

She shook her head and swiped the back of her hand across her nose.

He sighed. "Don't blame yourself. It isn't you. It's stuff that happened before you came. You couldn't know what you were getting into."

She swallowed hard, the lump in her chest swelling to unreal proportions.

He lifted his hands imploringly. "I've been thinking."

She nodded. "So have I."

He gave a crooked grin. "I'm sure of that. But let me say what I have to say first."

She wagged her head, unable to speak for fear of crying.

"I've been up all night." He paused.

She longed to ask about it but waited, letting him find his own way of telling her.

"I rode for awhile. All the way to town." His gaze grew dark, and he looked past her, to a place she couldn't go. "I went to Esther's grave, and I sat and thought a long time." His gaze returned to her, sharpening as he focused on her. "You're right. I need to talk to the boys."

She jerked like someone had yanked on her hair. She didn't know what she expected, but his sudden capitulation surprised her, and she stepped aside as he reached around her for the doorknob.

"Boys," he called out the door. "Come here."

The boys hurried inside.

Zach sat down. "Come here." He drew the boys to his knees and faced them squarely, looking at each solemn face for a long time.

Irene quietly sat down, unashamedly interested in the proceedings.

Zach touched Donald's face, running his hand under the boy's chin, pressing his thumb to the blunt little nose. "It's time we had a family talk." He turned to Harry, his big fist closing over the thin shoulder. "Some bad things happened to the three of us, and we need to talk about them to make sure you're all right."

Harry pressed closer to Zach's knees. Irene could feel the tension in him. Donald's gaze, dark and unblinking, bored into his father's.

Zach nodded as if they had spoken. "I know it must have scared you when your mama died."

Harry shuddered.

Zach continued. "I want you to know it wasn't your fault. It had nothing to do with you."

Harry looked like he would explode if he held himself any tighter. Donald's eyes were far too large for his face.

Irene edged her chair closer and pulled Donald to her lap,

holding him close, letting him face his dad as Zach continued to talk.

"Your mama got very sick, and no one knew in time to help her." He sought Irene's gaze as if begging for help. She nodded encouragement. He continued. "Maybe she said or did things when she was sick that made you think she didn't love you anymore."

Donald shuddered. Irene closed her eyes and took a deep breath. Had Zach suspected this all along?

"But she loved you right to the end."

Silence hung around them, filled with tension and unanswered questions.

"She made us stay in our room," Harry whispered.

Zach pulled the shivering boy into his lap. "Why did she do that?"

"Because we were bad. We made too much noise."

Irene could bear the child's pain no longer and edged closer, so she could wrap one arm around him.

Zach gave her a desperate, pleading look, silently begging for help in dealing with this child's confession.

She gave a tiny nod. "Can you remember what she said, Sweetheart?" Irene asked the shivering child.

"She said she was too tired to look after two noisy boys and said to stay in our room and play quietly."

"Don't you see? She was so sick she couldn't take care of you properly. Poor Mama."

Harry digested the information. "She was mad at us."

Irene shook her head. "I don't think so. But she was too sick to be able to tell you. I think she made you stay in your room because she wanted you to be safe." She pressed her face to his hair, tears stinging her eyes.

"Why did she throw out Donald's bear?"

Irene drew back, studying the demanding eyes. "I don't know. You'll have to tell me what bear you mean and what happened."

"You know, Donald's bear?"

"You mean the stuffed toy he brought me to fix?"

He nodded. "He took it to her when she was so tired." He and Donald looked at each other. The little boy on her lap tensed as he and his brother shared a secret memory, then Harry tipped his face to Irene. "He wanted her to feel better."

Irene nodded, squeezing the boy she held. "What happened?"

"Mommy shouted at him to leave her alone." He struggled with his thoughts and shuddered again. "Then she threw it out the window and told him to never bring it in again."

Zach groaned.

Irene blinked, unable to meet Zach's eyes, barely able to contain the pain that went on and on like a great, wild wind inside her.

"But how did Donald get it?"

Harry shrugged. "I don't know." He studied his brother, then smiled slowly. "I guess he sneaked out and hid it somewhere." He took Donald's hand. "Pretty smart, Donald."

Harry struggled with another question. "Do mommies and daddies always get sick?"

"Not very often."

"Your mommy died." His eyes accused her.

"Yes, but my daddy is still alive. And most of my friends still have a mommy and daddy, and they're all quite grown-up now. In fact, most of them have children of their own, and still their parents are alive and well." No need to tell the child how the war had upset many a home with losses, often of sons and young husbands.

"Will you get sick?"

Irene managed a little chuckle. "I don't imagine I will. I haven't been sick a day in my life."

He nodded, apparently satisfied, and turned to demand of Zach, "Will you get sick and die?"

Zach grunted. "Not if I can help it. I hate being sick. Yuck."

Harry giggled.

Irene stroked his hair. "Things happen that none of us plan. We can't promise you we will never get hurt or sick, but I promise if we do, we'll be sure to explain it to you so you know it's not your fault." She met Zach's eyes over the child's head, silently making him agree to the promise.

Harry sighed. "I guess that's all right then." He touched her face. "I'm glad you're my new mommy."

"Me, too," she managed around the lump in her throat. A tear trickled down her cheek as she hugged the boys closer. Zach's muscular arms wrapped them all together in one big hug. Donald squeezed in tight against her chest as they all enfolded him.

"Too squishy," a thin voice protested.

Zach loosened his grasp as Irene drew back. All of them stared at Donald.

"Did you say that, Son?" Zach demanded.

Donald nodded.

Zach jumped to his feet, tossing Donald high over his head. "That's my boy!" He shook Donald until a deep-throated chuckle escaped the boy. Zach held him in his arms, and father and son, dark eyes matching, stared at each other. Donald's expression remained solemn, but his twinkling eyes gave him away. Zach grinned widely. "Donald Marshall, it is so good to hear your voice again."

The little boy nodded solemnly.

Zach turned to face Irene. "Thank you," he whispered.

Her eyes brimming with tears, she shook her head. "You did it. You allowed them to be free."

"I wouldn't have done it without your prodding and your help. Thank you from the bottom of my heart."

Zach's happiness colored the day. He whooped, sweeping Donald into the air every time he entered the house. Irene knew he did it for the sheer joy of hearing Donald's chuckle.

When they sat down to supper, Zach bowed his head and added a special prayer of thanks to his customary grace.

He grinned at the boys as he passed them the bowl of tiny new potatoes cooked in their skins. "This is the best day I've had in a long time thanks to you two."

Irene smiled as she watched Harry wriggle under the warmth of his father's wide grin. The boy seemed to have shed a layer of worry before her eyes.

Donald watched as Zach spooned three tiny potatoes on his plate, then lifted his face and demanded, "More."

Zach roared with laughter. "Have you been starving to death all this time rather than say something?"

Donald nodded solemnly, his little pink tongue licking his lips as Zach added several more potatoes to the child's plate.

By bedtime, Irene knew the children were exhausted, the emotions unleashed this day having drained them.

"What would you like me to read to you tonight?" she asked them.

Donald ran and got her favorite book.

"You like this one, do you?"

He nodded as he handed it to her.

She ruffled his hair. "I think you'll remain a man of few words."

He nodded again.

Harry grinned at his brother. As they played outside this afternoon, Irene had stood at the window, watching and listening. As usual, Harry carried on a one-sided conversation, but occasionally, she caught a word or two uttered by Donald. And her heart overflowed.

Shortly after the boys were tucked in, Irene stifled a huge yawn. The day had left her exhausted. "I think I'll go to bed."

Zach sat reading and nodded as she left.

In the bedroom, she leaned against the window, looking out at the garden, now barely discernable in the dark shadows of the trees. A bird called a note, then fell silent. The abundance of the sweet peas filled the evening air with a heady scent that left her feeling empty. It was stupid. Considering all that had happened today, she should be supremely happy. And she was. She rejoiced that the boys had faced their memories. She wasn't naive enough to imagine they wouldn't have to deal with their past again and again, but today they had taken the first step.

And to hear Donald talk and laugh—she held the joy of the moment to her heart. It was the dearest thing she could have asked for.

Except for one thing—one selfish thing. She wanted Zach's love with a hunger that edged over her joy.

She pushed herself away from the window and prepared for bed, knowing Zach must be tired and waiting to get to sleep. She crawled under the blankets and opened her Bible, then looked up, startled when the door edged open and Zach came in.

Irene felt her eyes grow wide with shock.

Acting as if his actions were perfectly normal, he flopped down atop the covers.

She watched him, nervousness ticking inside her chest. What did he want?

But he lay staring up at the ceiling. "I can't begin to tell you how good it was to hear Donald speak again."

She could feel his barely contained tension.

He laughed low in his throat. "I feel a bit like Donald. Like I finally found my voice." Suddenly, he turned and impaled her with his dark gaze. "I think it did me as much good to talk about what happened as it did the boys."

She nodded, her voice trapped inside the tightness that had become her body.

"And I have you to thank for it."

"I didn't do anything," she protested, her voice breathless.

He touched her cheek. "You made me face a few facts. You made it possible for me to realize I needed to let go of some things and let God fill those places with His love." His finger trailed down her cheekbone and around her chin.

His eyes darkened. Then he tweaked her nose and turned on his back. "What are you doing?" He nodded toward her Bible.

She pulled together her scattered thoughts. "Reading my Bible."

"Read a chapter to me," he demanded.

She wet her lips and focused her skittish brain on the words before her. At first her words were stiff, almost stammering, then her voice smoothed out, and she read steadily to the end.

"Thanks for everything." He squeezed her hand, then jumped up and strode from the room, murmuring, "Good night," before he pulled the door shut.

She lay staring at the door, speechless at his behavior. For a minute, she had thought he was going to kiss her, declare his love—but all he did was thank her for forcing him to talk to the boys. "Anyone could have done that," she muttered to herself. She pressed her fingers to her cheek, following the tingling trail Zach had left. She soared at the memory of his touch, but crashed again as she contemplated his sudden departure. The whole thing was far too unsettling.

She pulled her hands from her face. It was no use fooling herself. He had made his decision plain from the very beginning. It was she who had changed. And she might as well change right back. A marriage of convenience was what she had agreed to, she reminded herself. Why couldn't she just be satisfied with the arrangement instead of longing for more? But even as she argued the point, the ache deepened until she groaned. She turned the lantern off, grateful Zach didn't return until she had calmed herself and was able to lie still and quiet when he finally crawled under the covers.

The next morning, Zach grabbed Donald and plunked him onto a chair. "Ready for breakfast, big man?"

"Unhuh."

Donald's grunt elicited a shout of laughter from his father. He caught Harry in his arm and swung the boy off his feet, landing him on the chair next to Donald. "So did that little brother of yours keep you awake all night with his chattering?"

Harry grinned, amused at his father's nonsense. "He's still a man of few words," Harry said and nodded.

Zach laughed, catching Irene's eye. "Your new mama understands us pretty well, doesn't she?" He regarded his sons. The three of them grinned at each other.

Over breakfast, Zach asked Irene, "What are your plans for the day?"

"Nothing special. I'll check the beans, and if they're ready to pick I will can some. Or maybe I'll do some weeding. Why?"

He dragged his gaze away from the boys. "Because we're going on a picnic."

Harry interrupted with a shout. "Yay!"

Zach laughed, then turned back to Irene. "How about we leave right after dinner and have a picnic supper. Is that all right with you?"

Irene nodded. "I'll be ready." She studied the three smiling faces. "I think we'll have a fine time."

She was glad for the time to prepare food and pick the beans to can tomorrow, but the boys could barely contain themselves.

"Is it dinnertime yet?" Harry asked for the hundredth time.

"Soon," Irene murmured. "Why don't you go find me a clean box to put the supper in?"

He raced out to the shed with Donald on his heels but was back in a matter of minutes. "Is this good enough?"

"It will do fine." She piled the sandwiches and cake in carefully while Harry and Donald bounced at her side, silently willing her to hurry. "I can't make time go any faster," she protested.

Harry sank into a chair. "I know."

"But I'll tell you what. Set the table, then run and find your dad. We'll eat early."

The boys needed no second invitation. They scurried about putting out dishes and cutlery, then raced outside to find Zach.

She heard them returning, Zach laughing as he rough-housed with them. She smiled at their noise. How good it was to hear them laughing and playing together.

"Where are we going?" Harry demanded as Zach turned the wagon westward.

"How'd you like to go to the river?"

"Great," Harry replied.

"River?" Donald asked.

Zach ruffled his hair. "Yes, young man, the river. You can

go wading or climb trees or throw rocks. Whatever you like."

"Good," Harry said, his eyes sparkling.

"Good," Donald echoed, crossing his arms in perfect imitation of Harry's stance.

Chuckling, Irene met Zach's gaze over the boys' heads. Her heart almost stalled at the warm depth of it. She fought a sudden impulse to sing. Then Zach turned to Harry as the boy explained to Donald how to skip rocks.

They pulled in under a canopy of trees, the dappled shade cool and moist. Zach leapt to the ground and swung the boys down before he reached up and lifted Irene to her feet. "Isn't this grand?" he asked. She agreed without knowing if he meant the weather, the day, or life in general and decided he probably meant them all; he fairly bubbled with joy.

He allowed the boys to pull him to the shore of the river, looking over his shoulder once to make sure Irene followed. Then the three of them had a rock-throwing contest. Harry had developed a deadly aim. "I see you've been practicing." Zach grunted and threw a rock across the water. "You've developed a good throw."

Harry's chest swelled with pride.

Then Zach's attention was drawn to his younger son as Donald grabbed his arm. "Watch," the boy demanded.

Irene settled on the grassy bank, her back against a tall pine and watched the trio. They seemed completely absorbed in each other. She knew they were unconsciously trying to make up for lost time. Despite her pleasure in their unity and healing, she felt shut out. She shook her head, dismayed at her selfishness. She had prayed for this to happen. She should feel nothing but gratitude.

Zach plopped down at her feet. "You're awfully quiet."

"Just content," she said. And it was suddenly true.

"Come on." He jumped up and grabbed her hand.

She let him pull her to her feet. When he retained her hand, she felt the last of her unsettledness flee.

"Come on, boys. I've got something to show you." He led them along the river until it widened.

Harry saw it first. "A boat!" He jumped up and down. "Can we go for a ride?"

"That's what I had in mind."

"Goody!" Harry yelled.

"Goody!" Donald echoed.

It was a wide, flat boat, large enough to seat six comfortably. Zach handed Irene in first so she could sit at one end. The two boys sat in the middle seat. Zach shoved the boat away from shore and jumped in, facing Irene. He unlocked the oars and rowed, grinning at them all. For a minute, she thought he would burst his buttons, he looked so proud. He gave her a look brimming with gratitude.

She nodded and smiled, but when he turned his attention back to his sons, she looked down over the side of the boat, trailing her fingers in the water. She did not resent his happiness in his sons. She did not even mind being shut out by their love for each other. But she did not want his gratitude. It wasn't enough. She wanted his love.

They rowed down the river, Zach pointing out different things. "It wasn't so long ago that explorers and fur traders paddled up and down this river."

"And Indians?" Harry asked.

"Indians, too, I'm sure." He grinned lopsidedly at Irene. "You see our country is still new and raw, not like England."

Harry turned to study her as if trying to picture her in a different country. "Did you go rowing in England?"

She nodded, smiling as she remembered. "Yes, we certainly did. Ladies in white lawn dresses and big straw hats with their beaus trying to impress them with their skill and strength. Sometimes they'd let the boat drift while the young men played a banjo or sang for his fair maiden. And there were fine lawns and lots of flowers along the edge of the lake."

"Like you and Daddy?" Harry regarded her with wide, curious eyes.

"How do you mean, like me and Daddy?"

"The young ladies and their—what did you call them?"

"Beaus?" she supplied.

"Yes. Beaus. Is that like you and Daddy?"

Her grin grew wide. She could feel the sparkle in her eyes. "Look at your daddy. Do you think he needs to prove how strong he is?" Two little heads turned toward Zach. Two little heads shook back and forth in answer to her question. "Me neither." An imp of mischief took control of her mind. "Though perhaps he could sing for us."

Zach shot her a half amused, half annoyed look. Then to her surprise and delight, he began singing in a low, deep voice, "Don't sit under the apple tree with anyone else but me."

A deep, warm glow began in the pit of her stomach and spread upward like a low flame licking at wood.

It wasn't until Zach jumped from the boat and pushed it the last few feet to shore that she realized they were back where they'd begun. Her palm tingling at his touch, she allowed him to help her from the boat, grateful that he dropped her hand immediately so he could secure the boat. She rubbed her hand against the material of her dress, trying desperately to settle her nerves into a semblance of order.

"Who's hungry?"

"We are!" Harry yelled, and the boys raced back down the trail toward the wagon.

Zach waited for Irene to fall in beside him. Thankfully, his attention was on the boys, and he didn't notice her nervous movements. By the time they reached the little clearing, Irene had her emotions firmly in control and had persuaded herself not to let them get away from her again.

Zach lifted the box from the wagon; Irene spread the quilt. Their hands brushed as they both reached to set out the food. Her nerve endings felt raw and oversensitive, as if she'd stepped too close to the fire.

She ducked her head and busied herself with distributing sandwiches and glasses of water. Zach, for his part, seemed not to notice. She smiled as she handed Harry another sandwich.

Why should Zach notice? She somehow managed to

maintain a calm, almost detached exterior while her insides boiled and churned like water in the washing machine when Harry pumped it back and forth.

Slowly, calmness settled through her. It was a lesson she'd learned long ago; act like you want to feel and soon you'll feel like you act. Or almost so.

The boys finished eating and wandered down to the water's edge.

"Don't get too close and fall in," Zach warned as he settled with his back against the trunk of a tree. He locked his fingers behind his neck and let out a long sigh. "I guess I really had forgotten how to have fun."

"It takes time to heal," Irene muttered, studiously keeping her gaze on her hands.

"Time and a little prodding, perhaps."

She could hear the amusement and gratitude in his voice. She could not look at him for fear he would see the hunger of her heart. Gratitude was great, she supposed. It simply didn't satisfy.

"Irene, come and sit down. Relax. It's a holiday." He patted the ground beside him.

Her hands clenched into tight fists. If she refused, he would demand to know what the problem was, yet she feared she could not sit so close and retain her composure.

Slowly, almost against her will, she turned to meet his eyes, dark insisting eyes, sparkling with his newfound joy. She swallowed loudly, unable to tear her gaze away.

Again he patted the ground beside him. "Come on."

She nodded and scuttled toward him, knowing she entered a danger zone, yet drawn inexplicably by his smile. She knew she should run while she could—run from her own emotions, run from the risk of revealing too much and turning him against her. But she could no more stop herself than she could swim back to England.

She pressed her back to the rough bark, keeping several inches between them. But he would have none of it. He dropped his arm across her lap and tucked her close to his side.

"There, that's better." He sat back with all the confidence of a man content with his world, grinning at her while her nerves twitched.

"Look," Harry called, pulling Zach's attention back to the boys. "I skipped a rock."

Irene let her breath ease out over her teeth and forced herself to relax. All those times of hiding her emotions as she worked in the hospital enabled her to order her body to appear calm.

"Good job," Zach called, his voice rumbling through her, stirring alive all the emotions she'd managed to calm.

She bit the inside of her lip and deliberately forced herself to concentrate on the boys' activities and called, "You try now, Donald." Cheering the boys provided an outlet for her riotous emotions.

"Throw like this." Zach called instructions to Donald, lifting his arm and pulling it back to illustrate.

It was more than she could bear, and she sprang to her feet. "Say, weren't we promised we could go wading?" She slipped off her shoes and stockings and gathered up her skirt. "Last one in is a rotten egg."

The boys struggled to remove shoes and socks before she reached them. She raced past, splashing water over them.

"Come on, Dad," Harry yelled.

Irene thought Zach might refuse, but he rolled up his pant legs and headed for the water.

Zach and the boys stood ankle deep in the water, not moving.

Irene faced them, several feet out, the water to her calves. "You're supposed to play in it," she called, scooping up a handful of water and tossing it at the threesome.

Harry laughed, licking water drops from his face, then bent over and skimmed his fingers over the water, sending a spray over Donald.

Donald giggled and jumped up and down, making little waves.

Zach grunted. "Play, huh?" He plowed through the water toward Irene.

Guessing his intention, she squealed and tried to escape, but she only got a few feet before his arms wrapped around her, crushing her to his chest. She struggled. "Let me go."

He lifted her off her feet.

She kicked at the water, splashing as hard as she could.

He held her out, silently threatening to dunk her.

"You wouldn't dare." His eyes were so close, so intense, she could barely speak, but the threat of being dunked overcame all other emotions.

"Wouldn't I?" his breath whispered over her.

She began to struggle, trying to regain her footing, squealing as he loosened his hold. She grabbed his shirt and held on.

His arms tightened around her, pulling her to his chest. Their faces inches apart, she could see the darkening purpose in his eyes. Her insides calmed. Nothing else existed. She strained toward him, lifting her face, silently asking for his kiss.

"You're not going to hurt her, are you, Dad?" Harry's voice thinned with worry.

Zach froze. He blinked, and his arms slowly released her until she stood in the water, still clutching his arm.

"No, I wouldn't hurt her." Their gazes locked. He looked deep into her eyes, promising her something. She blinked and pulled away. Was it a promise not to hurt her? Was it a promise to be grateful? She churned her way back to shore. It wasn't enough. She wanted more. She wanted it all.

twelve

Irene heard the boys playing in the hallway as she did dishes but gave it little thought. They seldom got into mischief.

"Dad, come here," Harry called.

Zach drank the last of his coffee and strode across the room to join the boys, their mumbled conversation muted.

Curious, Irene went to the doorway to see what they were doing. The three of them sat on the floor before the big chest, the boys leaning across Zach's knees. Harry picked a picture from the stack and handed it to Zach. He nodded and, in low tones, talked about it. Irene watched for a moment. A deep contentment swelled within her. She was glad they had found their way back to each other.

But her joy was tainted and troubled by her selfishness. She wanted it all. She wanted his home, his family, and his love.

In an attempt to rid herself of her traitorous thoughts, she heated water and began scouring the walls although they didn't need cleaning.

Suddenly, Harry stood before her. She jerked back, startled by his appearance. He watched her guardedly, a framed picture clutched in his hands. "Dad said we could put out some of the pictures if you don't mind."

Donald at his side, Zach stood in the doorway, his expression guarded.

"I think it's a wonderful idea." She dried her hands. "What do you have?"

Harry handed her the picture. "It's me as a baby."

"I'd love to be able to look at this every day. Where would you like to put it?" She led the way into the front room and waited while Harry looked around, solemnly choosing the best place. Finally, he set it on the narrow table next to the clock.

"What about you, Donald?"

Donald stepped forward and handed her the picture of himself as a baby. "It's me."

"It certainly is. Where would you like it?"

He set it next to Harry's picture.

She crossed her arms and studied the pictures. "Aren't there more?"

Harry darted a glance toward his father, then nodded. "We didn't know if you would want Mommy's picture out to look at all the time."

Acutely aware of Zach's dark gaze on her, Irene met Harry's gaze steadily. She could feel the waiting in the room. "I don't think I'd mind. Why should you think I might?"

Harry's gaze was so intense. "Because you're our new mommy now." He considered his answer and added, "And we didn't want you to think we weren't glad."

"Oh, Harry. That's so sweet." She bent and hugged him. "But I don't ever want you to forget your first mommy. That would be wrong. After all, she loved you very much. You should always remember that. And if a picture helps you remember, then I'm glad for you." She straightened, keeping her eyes turned away from Zach. She didn't want any more gratitude. She acted out of love only and only wanted love in return. Gratitude was an insipid substitute. "Why don't you run and get a picture to put here?"

Harry pulled Donald after him.

"That was very kind."

She spun on him, anger blazing through her. "I love them. Why wouldn't I be kind?"

He blinked. "I didn't mean it that way."

"Then how did you mean it? You act like it's strange I should care about how they feel—how you feel. Did you think I could care for everyone and not feel something for them?" Breathing hard, she forced herself to stop before she said more than she wanted.

His eyes narrowed. "I didn't think anything of the sort. I was only thinking you shouldn't have to feel like you're a substitute for Esther. Isn't that what you want? Haven't you told me often enough you couldn't do that? You didn't want to?"

Her anger fled as quickly as it came. "I'm sorry. I didn't mean to explode like that. And thank you for thinking about my feelings."

The boys returned before Zach could answer. Irene took her time at placing Zach and Irene's wedding picture. She truly didn't mind having Esther's picture for the boys to look at, but it stung more than she could have imagined to see Zach smiling down at her like that. Esther had had it all—she'd had his love. Studying the adoration on Zach's face, she admitted defeat. Zach had loved Esther so completely, he would never love another. Something inside her fizzled and died. Slowly, she turned. She met Zach's gaze and smiled, her eyes feeling flat and lifeless. "I better finish up my mess." She edged past Zach to the kitchen.

He lifted his hand as if to detain her, but she slipped away. She couldn't face him right now.

"Come on, boys. I need you to help me with something," Zach said.

Irene was grateful to hear them all traipse outside. As soon as they left, she fled to the bedroom, falling on her knees beside the bed. Scalding tears poured down her cheeks. She dashed them away. "Oh, God," she whispered, "I wanted so much more than anyone offered. And I've let my feelings get in the way. Help me be able to show my love in the way I care for Zach and the boys. Help me be satisfied with that."

Zach and the boys didn't return until dinnertime. By then, Irene had settled in her mind that her love would find its satisfaction in serving generously, in giving love without expecting it to be returned, and she was able to greet their return with a warm smile. "What have you been doing all morning?" she asked.

Harry and Donald exchanged looks. "Can't tell you," Harry said solemnly.

Irene grinned. "Is it a guessing game?"

The boys shook their heads.

"I see." She tried to catch Zach's eyes, but he seemed terribly interested in buttering a slice of bread. "Very well. Ask me what I did this morning."

"What?" The boys were obviously curious. Even Zach's hands grew still as he listened.

"Well. I had a very interesting day." She drawled the words out. "I picked a bouquet of flowers." She pointed to the jar on the counter. "I discovered that our roses are thriving." She grabbed the jar. "See, these roses are from our bushes."

Harry jumped from his chair. "I want to see."

"After dinner," Zach ordered.

Harry settled back to his meal.

"Roses are blooming, huh?" Zach gave her a long, steady look.

Irene nodded. "The bushes are loaded."

"That must be a good omen."

"I suppose." She had no idea what he meant and turned away from his dark gaze, determined to keep a tight rein on her emotions.

As soon as they were done eating, Zach stood and waved the two boys to his side. "Come along. We have work to do."

"Can I see the roses first?" Harry asked.

"We'll go by them before we go back to work."

Irene watched as the trio traipsed to the bushes. Despite their scrawny appearance, the plants were covered in various shades of pink blossoms, some almost white, some as dark pink, almost red.

The three of them stood talking and gesturing for a few minutes, then marched off toward the barn. Irene smiled, content that they were enjoying each other, then turned her attention to the beets she had boiled early in the day intending to pickle them.

She had poured the hot, spicy vinegar solution over the sliced beets and set them to seal when Zach and the boys burst into the house. They were fairly bouncing with excitement.

"We have a surprise for you," Harry announced.

"You do?" Her gaze slid from one to the other, and she almost tripped at the intensity in Zach's eyes.

"Yes," Donald announced, his eyes sparkling.

"Sit down." Harry led her to a chair. "Now wait here." He turned and rushed outside, Donald hot on his heels. Zach leaned against the door, his arms crossed over his chest, a slow easy smile creasing his face. Irene tore her gaze from him to watch the doorway.

The boys returned, holding a large, flat object between them. "We made it," Harry announced and set the object on her knees.

Irene gasped. Tears sprang to her eyes. It was a wooden picture; the words "Irene-Mommy" carved across it were encircled by a collection of buttons in all shapes and sizes and bows made from an assortment of ribbons and yard goods. "It's beautiful." She could barely speak around the tears clogging her throat, and she dashed away one that trickled down her cheek.

Donald and Harry leaned against her, one on either side. "It's all buttons and bows," Harry said. "To show you we're glad you're our new mommy."

She drew them to her. "I am, too." She kissed each head. "I love you both. Very much."

"I love you, too," Harry said.

"Me, too," Donald echoed, planting a wet kiss on her cheek.

Her eyes blurred with tears. She looked to Zach, her heart overflowing. "Thank you," she whispered.

"No. Thank you." He leaned forward, using his thumb to wipe a tear from her face. A shudder of pleasure and longing swept over her. She hoped he would think it was only a sob.

His face close, he spoke low, his deep voice shivering through her. "I praise God He sent you into our lives. Remember when you said you wanted to live up to your name—bringer of peace?"

She nodded.

"Well, you have. You've brought peace. I am grateful to you and God."

She couldn't speak.

"Where will you put it?" Harry demanded.

She gave him a tremulous smile. She glanced around the room, then nodded toward the wall next to the hall. "How about right there where I can see it every day?"

Zach straightened. "I'll get the hammer and nail."

A few minutes later, the picture was hung, and they all stood back to admire it. "It's the nicest present I ever had," Irene said.

"Really?" Harry demanded.

"Really." She leaned over and kissed his cheek, then Donald's. Donald's arms wrapped around her neck and held her tight while he kissed her.

"We better let your mommy finish her work." Zach led the boys outside.

"Thank you," she called after them.

But she didn't go back to work. Instead, she stared at the picture, knowing this was reward enough for loving Zach in secret. At least she could love the boys openly. Then, smiling, determined to give her love freely, she turned to prepare the evening meal.

Yet, despite her resolve, as she prepared for bed, she wished for more. Under the cover of darkness, Zach crawled into bed. She ached for him to take her in his arms, to pull her close. To say he loved her even a little. . . She longed to be more than a mother for his boys, a keeper of his home, and a wife in name only. But he lay on his side of the bed. In a few minutes, his breathing deepened, and she knew he was asleep.

And so it remained day after day. He was kind, attentive even, and profoundly grateful. But nothing more.

❧

A week later, Addie drove into the yard. "I've come for the boys."

"What?" Irene stared.

Addie raised her eyebrows. "Zach didn't tell you?"

"Tell me what?"

"He made arrangements on Sunday for me to come and get the boys and keep them overnight."

"He did?"

Addie grinned. "I guess it's a surprise. Where is he?"

"I'm not sure."

Addie glanced around. "Here he comes now." Zach strode up the side of the hill. "So, big brother, what is it you've got up your sleeve?"

Zach shot her an annoyed look. "None of your business."

Addie laughed. "I see. Never mind. I'll go find the boys."

Zach intercepted her. "I'll get them." He strode to the back of the house where the boys were playing, returning a few minutes later with the pair.

"Aunt Addie!" Harry yelled. "Dad says we can stay with you tonight."

"Won't that be fun?"

Harry nodded.

"Well, Donald," Addie said.

"Lo," he said.

Addie stared at him. "He said hello."

Zach laughed. "What did you expect him to say? Good-bye?"

She shot her brother a you-know-what-I-mean look. "It's nice to hear your voice again."

"Yup," Donald agreed.

Irene laughed. "He's still a man of few words."

Zach and Harry chuckled at their little secret.

"Come on, then." Addie loaded the boys into the wagon. Then she grinned down at Zach and Irene. "You two have a good time, now." Laughing, she drove away.

Irene stared after her, suddenly feeling very vulnerable.

Zach took her hand. "Come with me." He led her down the slope to the bottom of the valley, holding her hand to help her keep her footing on the steep slope.

She longed to ask what his plans were, but her heart forbade her. She wanted it to be one thing; perhaps he had something else in mind.

At the bottom of the hill, he led her to a small copse of trees. He parted the branches and led her to the clearing in the middle. Wild roses, harebells, and fragrant sweet clover had been cut and scattered around. She halted, staring at the scene, feeling like she'd stepped into space, not knowing where her next footstep would land.

"Don't be frightened," he whispered, pulling her into the clearing.

The scent of the flowers stirred her senses as did his warm hand.

"I only wanted a chance to be alone without two curious little boys interrupting so I could tell you how I feel." He grasped her chin between his finger and thumb, forcing her to meet his gaze. "I hope I'm not rushing you." His gaze slid down her face, lingering on her lips. "I thought maybe you guessed how I felt."

Irene blinked. "You're grateful."

"Grateful?" He seemed puzzled. "Of course I'm grateful, but that's not what I mean." He seemed befuddled as he stroked his thumb over her lips.

"What do you mean, then?"

He gave her a slow, lazy smile. He gazed deep into her soul. "Surely you've guessed."

Not daring to hope, she shook her head. "You'll have to tell me."

"If you insist." His voice held a bemused tone. For a moment, he was again distracted by his searching study of her face. "Irene, I've wanted to tell you this for ages, but every time I try, you turn away or the boys butt in. That's why I sent them to visit Addie for the day."

She stood as still as the sun in the sky, willing him to continue, allowing herself a tiny glimmer of hope.

"Irene, what I want to say is, I love you."

She sniffed as tears stung her nose.

His eyes narrowed. "I know we agreed on a marriage of convenience, but it didn't take me long to discover that wasn't enough." He stared into her eyes. "Irene, say something."

She couldn't speak. Her heart was too full. A chuckle began low in her throat and escaped, swelling into a shout of laughter.

Zach drew back an inch, puzzled by her reaction.

"Do you know how long I've thought the same thing, hating the words 'marriage of convenience'?" she chortled.

His eyes widened. "Are you saying—"

"That I love you?"

He nodded.

"Yes, yes, yes!" she shouted, throwing her arms around his neck. "I love you, Zachary Marshall."

His expression filled with wonder. "I love you, Irene Marshall." The smell of wild roses filled her senses as his lips covered hers, at first gentle and sweet, then more demanding.

She snuggled against him, silently thanking God. Now she had it all.

"All buttons and bows," he whispered against her lips.

"Indeed," she murmured before he kissed her.

A Letter To Our Readers

Dear Reader:

In order that we might better contribute to your reading enjoyment, we would appreciate your taking a few minutes to respond to the following questions. We welcome your comments and read each form and letter we receive. When completed, please return to the following:

Fiction Editor
Heartsong Presents
PO Box 719
Uhrichsville, Ohio 44683

1. Did you enjoy reading *Irene* by Linda Ford?
   ❑ Very much! I would like to see more books by this author!
   ❑ Moderately. I would have enjoyed it more if

   _____

   _____

   _____

2. Are you a member of **Heartsong Presents**?   ❑ Yes   ❑ No
   If no, where did you purchase this book? _____

   _____

3. How would you rate, on a scale from 1 (poor) to 5 (superior), the cover design? _____

4. On a scale from 1 (poor) to 10 (superior), please rate the following elements.

   _____ Heroine   _____ Plot
   _____ Hero   _____ Inspirational theme
   _____ Setting   _____ Secondary characters

5. These characters were special because?_____

_____

_____

6. How has this book inspired your life?_____

_____

_____

7. What settings would you like to see covered in future
   Heartsong Presents books? _____

_____

_____

8. What are some inspirational themes you would like to see
   treated in future books? _____

_____

_____

9. Would you be interested in reading other **Heartsong
   Presents** titles?   ❏ Yes   ❏ No

10. Please check your age range:
    ❏ Under 18   ❏ 18-24
    ❏ 25-34   ❏ 35-45
    ❏ 46-55   ❏ Over 55

Name_____

Occupation_____

Address_____

City_____ State_____ Zip_____

Heartsong

HISTORICAL ROMANCE IS CHEAPER BY THE DOZEN!

Any 12 Heartsong Presents titles for only $27.00*

Buy any assortment of twelve *Heartsong Presents* titles and save 25% off of the already discounted price of $2.97 each!

*plus $2.00 shipping and handling per order and sales tax where applicable.

HEARTSONG PRESENTS TITLES AVAILABLE NOW:

(If ordering from this page, please remember to include it with the order form.)